Praise for *White Ghost Girls:*

"An auspicious debut sensitively and impressionistically evokes adolescent turmoil in Vietnam War–era Hong Kong. Greenway vividly conjures the fears, passions and fantasies of a teenager against a heart-rending political background. Assured, sensuous, brilliantly colored." —*Kirkus Reviews* (starred review)

"This is a novel about memory and loss, and most of all, yéarning. Greenway is a remarkable young writer who vividly evokes Hong Kong's sights, smells, and sounds ('the single chime of a high-pitched temple bell, the knocking of a wooden fish') in poetic, finely detailed prose. What's more, she seems to have remembered every single charged emotion from adolescence and filters them all through the sisters' fierce, complex relationship. A heartbreakingly beautiful debut." —*Booklist* (starred review)

"For all its dreamy lyricism, this debut novel about two teenage American sisters growing up in Hong Kong one summer boasts a satisfyingly complicated plot and a devastating conclusion. Along with death and sex, Greenway makes the illicit excitement of war and the sisters' opposing natures inextricably entwined."
—*Publishers Weekly*

"[The sisters'] intense bond, which draws them together while pitting them against each other, is brilliantly wrought, as is the era's political upheaval, which comes into sharp focus as the pair struggles to delineate friend from foe. As Frankie and Kate proceed to unravel life's rhythm and mysteries, Hong Kong itself becomes a third character. Greenway, an American reared in Asia and the Middle East, has created a compelling, heartbreaking and original first novel."
—*Library Journal*

"A haunting first novel written with the craft and grace of a master. Don't miss it!"   —Isabel Allende

"Alice Greenway writes of the violence at the heart of things. She is interested in the poetry and the horror, which is the rich, solemn, and subversive life of a young girl, reminding us of the taut balance between the civilized self and the hidden self."   —Susanna Moore

"Alice Greenway's white ghost girls are stunning characters and this novel is a stunning debut—ferocious, sensual, witty, elegantly wrought. The scene is Hong Kong in the summer of 1967, and the girls are expatriate teenagers navigating adolescence and violent political upheaval all at once. But the true subject of the book is neither adolescence nor political but longing, and the grief that follows. This short novel can be read at a sitting and, once read, is unforgettable."   —Ward Just

"Alice Greenway's *White Ghost Girls* is a ravishingly beautiful novel about sisters and about memory and about loss. And, as only true works of art can do, in focusing on the personal story, it brightly illuminates a great political and historical issue: *White Ghost Girls* gives us an utterly surprising and deeply resonant view of the American war in Vietnam. Heartbreakingly beautiful, richly sensual, this is a truly exciting debut novel by an extraordinarily talented new writer."   —Robert Olen Butler

"*White Ghost Girls* is a lovely book, graceful, poignant, and precise. It's about memory and love and homesickness, and how war will tear a family apart from afar."   —Roxana Robinson

White
Ghost
Girls

White Ghost Girls

ALICE GREENWAY

BLACK CAT
New York
a paperback original imprint of Grove/Atlantic, Inc.

First published in Great Britain in 2006 by
Atlantic Books, an imprint of Grove Atlantic Ltd.

Printed in the United States of America
Published simultaneously in Canada

FIRST AMERICAN EDITION

Library of Congress Cataloging-in-Publication Data
Greenway, Alice.
    White ghost girls / Alice Greenway.
       p. cm.
    ISBN 0-8021-7018-8
    1. Runaway teenagers—Fiction. 2. War photographers—Family
relationships—Fiction. 3. Americans—China—Fiction. 4. Hong Kong (China)—
Fiction. 5. Teenage girls—Fiction. 6. Sisters—Fiction. I. Title.
    PS3607.R4683W48 2006
    813'.6—dc22   2005052750

Black Cat
a paperback original imprint of Grove/Atlantic, Inc.
841 Broadway
New York, NY 10003

06 07 08 09 10   10 9 8 7 6 5 4 3 2 1

To Timo, Annie and Eliza,
and in memory of Theodore,
with all my love.

one

What can you give me?

Can you give me a back alley, a smoke-filled temple where white-hooded mourners burn offerings and wail for the dead? The single chime of a high-pitched temple bell? The knocking of a wooden fish?

Can you give me hot rain, mould-streaked walls, a sharpness that creeps into my clothes, infests my books? The smells of dried oysters, clove hair oil, tiger balm, joss burning to Kuan Yin in the back room of a Chinese amah? The feverish shriek of cicadas, the cry of black-eared kites? The translucent green of sun shining through elephant ear leaves?

Can you give me a handful of coloured silk? An empty pack of cigarettes? A tape recorder? Narrow, stepped streets, balconies hung with shop signs, laundry strung on bamboo poles, rattan birdcages? A ripened pomelo split open? The chalky bone of cuttlefish?

Can you give me my father's hand in mine, Frankie's in the other? Then take everything and go away?

Because if you can't, it's not enough. And if you can, I might leave anyhow. I'll head for cover. Disappear in jungles of triple canopy.

~   ~   ~

Out in the harbour, at the end of summer, fishermen feed the hungry ghosts. They float paper boats shaped like junks and steamships. One is double-prowed like the cross-harbour Star Ferry which plies its way back and forth between Hong Kong and Kowloon, never having to turn around. The fishermen load each tiny paper boat with some tea leaves, a drop of cooking oil, a spoonful of rice, a splash of petrol before setting it afloat. Boats for the lost at sea, for the drowned. They hire musicians to clang cymbals. Children throw burning spirit-money into the waves.

This summer, the one I'm going to tell you about, is the only time that matters. It's the time I'll think of when I'm dying, just as another might recall a lost lover or regret a love they never had. For me, there is one story. It's my sister's – Frankie's.

~   ~   ~

'Touched you last,' Frankie taunts. She runs out across the beach. Arms waving, shouting Indian war whoops, she plunges into the warm, green waves. Dares me to follow. Shaking off the stupor of the heat, I dash out after her.

Inside our shack, it's hot and close. Rank smells of sea salt, mould, sand. Air so wet, it trickles down the creases of our skin. Pools collect in the bends of our arms, behind our knees. Waves lap. Cicadas shriek. Barnacles and snails, stranded above the tide line, clamp tightly to rocks.

Frankie feeds me roe she's extracted from the belly of a purple-spined sea urchin, the way the boatman Ah Wong has taught us. I lick the soft yellow eggs off her finger. The taste is raw and salty-smooth. It's how explorers, castaways survive: Magellan, Columbus, Crusoe, eating the flesh of wild sea turtles, mangy gulls. Sometimes we dive for rubbery black sea slugs. Frankie squeezes one, shooting me with a film of sticky innards. It's the creature's only means of defence. It takes them a full year to rearm.

~   ~   ~

We're already too old for this, our games of castaway. We take them up self-consciously. Construct our shacks of flotsam and jetsam: rope, tin, fishing-net, Styrofoam, driftwood. Drag our finds back from rocks along the shore, step barefoot on crusty barnacles, rough granite, through tidal pools harbouring crabs and limpets. At the back of the beach, sharp vines clasp at our skin: vitex, rattlebox, morning glory. They criss-cross our ankles with scratches and scabs. Calluses grow thick on the soles of our feet. Startled, an ungainly coucal crashes through the undergrowth. Its echoing, whooping cry sounds like a monkey rather than a bird.

Then again, it's in our nature to gather, to scavenge. My mother hoards tubes of paints, charcoal pencils, erasers, inks, pens. Stores them in art boxes and Chinese baskets piled in her room with hard blocks of watercolour paper. My father keeps war relics in his darkroom, treasures my mother doesn't like to see: slivers of shrapnel he dug out of his leg, a grenade pin, a smuggled AK-47 stashed under the basin. A string of tiny temple bells that jangle on the door so you have to open it slowly, carefully, if you don't want anyone to hear you. A thin, tattered Vietnamese–English dictionary.

Secretly foraging, Frankie and I discover the Vietnamese words for nationalism and People's Democratic Revolution, dialectic materialism and exploitation. We find words for blood transfusion, guerrilla warfare and napalm. A bomb exploded and killed many people: *Bom nổ giết chết nhiều người*. Words for utopia, *không tưởng*, and sexual intercourse, *giới tính*. We pronounce them phonetically, like witches' spells. We look at the pictures my father's taken. Photographs of war.

~   ~   ~

Secret sisters. Shipwrecked sisters. Viet Cong sisters is what we call ourselves.

Frankie's back is strong and dark. She ties her long brown hair in two braids. Although our mother pleads with her to wear a top, she swims only in cut-off shorts. Maybe she's not ready to grow up. More likely, she wants to upset our mother. Her breasts are already full and round, like mangosteens. They bounce when she runs. Voluptuous is the word McKenna used when he and my father last came out of Saigon. It made my mother wince.

Me, I am thinner, leaner. Miró or Giacometti, my mother calls me. My hair is fair and cropped like a boy. It mats to my head with sea salt. I wear a threadbare blue-and-white bikini, hiding pointy, childish nipples. My skin is sunburned. When my father takes photos of me, I stare straight at the camera. I am twelve, nearly thirteen.

'Come, Kate,' Frankie calls me from the sea. I sprint. Feet, knees, legs fly across the sand, batter through the warm water. A wave rises up and slaps hard against my chest, then sweeps back, scratching my ankles with island sand, pulls as if to drag me down. I dive.

Underwater, it's cooler, quieter, green-blue. Purple-black sea urchins cling to rocks. Rough-skinned starfish stretch their arms in every direction. Fish dart past, swept along by the wash of waves. A pink sea anemone shudders fleshy tentacles. I hear the throbbing whine of a boat engine, an ancient *kaido* ferrying passengers to Yung Shue Wan, on the opposite end of Lamma Island.

Frankie grins, swims off; her arms pull broad, strong strokes, skimming the sandy bottom. I swim as fast as I can, knowing I won't beat her. Hold my breath until my chest aches, then kick to the surface, gasp in air. Frankie is faster, bigger, stronger. But she's also more needy. She needs my participation, my surrender in order to assert herself.

Breathless, I flip over. Floating upward, I dip my head back so the water licks my forehead. My eyes squint in the sun. From here, our shack looks like one of the squatter huts that catch fire or collapse down the muddy slopes of Hong Kong in sudden landslips.

Or maybe it's a Cubist painting in one of my mother's art books: a collage of forgotten items tacked on a cork-board.

The Chinese believe dragons lie curled asleep under these hills. Construction of new roads, the digging of foundations for apartment buildings can cut into the creatures' flesh. The earth bleeds red ochre. Then the great beasts must be appeased, offerings made, to avoid disease, bankruptcy or sudden, unexplained death. These bare, knobby hills are a dragon's vertebrae, spinal humps that might plunge under at any time, sucking us down with them.

All Hong Kong's islands look this way. Their forests cut down for firewood and shipbuilding. Their fertile valleys flooded at the end of the Ice Age, leaving steep mountains jutting out of the sea.

two

'Kate. Frances,' my mother calls our names from the stern of the junk. I roll over in the water and watch her stand up under the shade of the boat's canvas awning. She slips an elastic band around her watercolour pad, gathers her paints and tucks them into a big rattan bag. Her blonde hair is clipped back with a tortoiseshell pin to keep it off her neck. She wears a light Indian cloth tied modestly over her bathing suit, like a sarong. It puzzles me how she can sit so long without jumping into the sea. How, when she swims, she keeps her head above water, to keep her hair dry, rather than diving into the deep.

Ah Wong, in full sun, winds his fishing-line around a hand-held wooden frame. We could swim back to the junk perfectly well but Ah Wong always brings the dinghy out to fetch us. Squatting at the bow, he rows with a single oar, swivelling it along one side of the boat, then the other.

I swim, slowly at first so Frankie won't notice, then faster. Now's my chance to beat her because I'm closer and Frankie has caught a ride with Ah Wong. Hitching her arms over the dinghy's transom, she lets her brown legs trail heavily through the water behind. She's pretending not to notice me or maybe she doesn't. I know it's silly but I'm choking with triumph as I pull myself up the anchor line, launch my body on to the hot deck. My toes stretch wide over the rough, thick rope. Sea water streams down my face into my mouth, drips from my legs making rivulets in the dry, sun-baked wood. When I stand, my stomach leaves a dark curved stain between the prow and anchor chock.

~   ~   ~

At first I am the only one who sees it. A dark spot deep in the water, hidden by twinkling waves. The sun's reflection searing a momentary speck on my retina. Only when I blink, it's still there.

'Cheater,' Frankie objects. As the dinghy nears, she unhooks her arms and slips back easily into the sea. 'I was much further out. You didn't call it.' She glares up at me, waits for me to defend myself, knowing she can undo me. Only I'm not looking at Frankie but beneath her, where the spot is growing, taking shape. A shadow, distinctly darker than the milk-jade sea that cradles it. Rising up beneath my sister.

Shark is what I'm scared of. Now I remember the two other junks that anchored at Sham Wan for picnic lunches. Regret how Frankie and I scowled at them from the inside of our shack, scorning the plump English children jumping off the bow, threatening to invade our world. Both junks left hours ago. If it's a shark, racing up with open jaws, we're all alone. My heart races. My asthmatic lungs suck in air. I should shout. I need to warn her. But I cannot. Maybe if I don't move, hold my breath, I can stop time.

'What is it?' Frankie demands, still cross about the race. Dazzled by the sea's bright surface, she ducks down, peers through the green.

Now Ah Wong sees it too. Swiftly, he brings the dinghy back

around. With his thin, sinewy arms, he hauls Frankie up like a huge, slippery fish.

'*Fai di. Fai di.*' Quickly, quickly.

The way the shadow hovers, floating up, it's like a jellyfish. In shape, an angel. But it's not until the body breaks the surface that I see it's dead, drowned.

~   ~   ~

Black hair, a tentacled halo, spreads along the ripples of the water's surface. Black rags, the clothes of a Chinese farmer, catch like seaweed. A sickly rot bursts upward, making us screw up our faces as we stare down from the two boats.

The body is swollen and bloated like a buoy. Like a dead pig I once saw floating in the harbour, its skin so tight I thought it might pop. Frankie scuttles to the centre of the dinghy as if afraid the corpse could reach out and touch her. She covers her mouth and nose with her hands. That close, the smell must be even stronger.

'It's a woman!' My mother's voice at my side startles me. I can see that for myself, where the clothes are torn, but I don't know if this makes it better or worse.

We're caught, rapt, unable to look away. It's as if we expect the body to roll over in the sea and speak, tell us her story. Instead she stares blankly, strangely expressionless, until I realize she has no eyeballs. In their place, her eye-sockets swarm with tiny white fish carried up from the deep. The fish thrash frenzied in the hot, bright sun but unwilling to let go the sweet, rotten strands of flesh.

Only Ah Wong knows what to do. Muttering, he pulls the dinghy alongside the junk while Frankie climbs up. Then retrieves a rope. Tying a quick noose, he loops it around the dead woman's feet and tows her body quickly to shore.

We should turn away, refuse to look. My mother orders us down into the cabin as if she could erase what we've seen. When we get back to Hong Kong, she'll call the police or the coast guard.

Down here, it's hot, it smells like diesel and pitch. Waves lick the hull. We hear Ah Wong return, hear him pull up the anchor, plunge it into the water to wash it clean, the sound of chain clanking on the deck, the deafening splutter of the engine roaring to life. A welcome waft of air cools us as the junk turns, heads out of the bay.

My mother throws up over the gunnel. She keeps her head covered with a towel, bent over a plastic bucket, all the way back to Aberdeen.

We should be sick too. Maybe that's why she sent us down into the airless cabin. Instead, we creep past her, assume our usual lookout at the prow, perching either side of the bowsprit. Looking back at the beach, I see the body stranded just above the tide line. Thrifty though he is, Ah Wong has left his rope.

'Christ, it stank,' Frankie says. Her words re-establish her composure, her command. Down in the cabin, she hasn't said a thing. Neither have I.

'You just stared, goggle-eyed. You should have seen yourself. God, I could have been eaten up by a giant squid.' Her eyes widen in imitation. She's teasing me. But at the same time, her voice trembles with eagerness and excitement. Her hot thigh presses against mine. Our salty shoulders brush.

'Secret sisters,' Frankie whispers.

'Secret sisters,' I reply. Our bodies quietly share the thrill of it, the repulsion. The sudden change in everything.

~   ~   ~

I didn't mean to begin here. I wanted to tell you about Frankie and me alone on the beach as we often were that summer. How we liked to sit at the bow of the boat, kick at the sea. I can feel it now, if I close my eyes, breathe deeply. The sea, the smell of dried fish, of cooking fires wafting from Chinese villages or passing junks. The warm wind fanning our hot bodies as the wooden boat rises and dips, ploughing its way back through the green. The slow darkening of sky and islands. How we dare the water to catch our feet, our shins, tug, up to our thighs, hissing, until the junk rears up again on the next wave and the sea lets go.

The body floats up in these pages the same way it did in the sea that day, unexpected, shocking. I see now, it's something we were waiting for.

The body changes us. That's why my mother doesn't want us to see it, is sick in a red bucket. It marks the end of our innocence, exposes the impossibility of her efforts to protect us.

We've seen what my father sees in Vietnam. Mined, napalmed, fire-bombed, shot, burned. We have a body now too. Drowned.

Three

My father knows about dead people. He photographs the war for *Time* magazine in New York.

In the morning, I spread the paper across the living-room table. There's a black-and-white photo of American soldiers wading through a stream lined with mangrove trees. The soldiers walk thigh-deep through the muddy water, equipment hanging off them, faces alert, guns bristling. I look for my father.

It's early but already hot. The French doors to the veranda open wide to let in the night air, which isn't any cooler. Frankie and I whisper so as not to wake my mother. We hear the splutter of junks returning from night fishing-grounds. Diesel engines cut in and out as they chug their way through the channel between Hong Kong and Lamma Island. Ah Bing sings, high-pitched, in her back room.

Our apartment's near Pok Fu Lam village. We rent the middle floor of a three-storey, slightly greying stucco house. Below us, Mr Mok, our landlord, lives on the ground floor. Above us, the *taitais*, the three elderly wives of his late father. We're the cheese in the sandwich, my father says. A buffer for Mr Mok. But it's because of the trees that my father chose the apartment. The trees and the view west over Lamma, Cheung Chau and Lantau islands.

'Just wait until you see it, Marianne, the flame of the forest trees, the jade-green sea,' my father crowed when he came to collect us from New York two summers ago. Hong Kong would be safer than Saigon; an old-fashioned British enclave, he called it. That was before the trouble started this summer.

My father was sent to Vietnam in time to photograph the Marines landing on the beach at Danang, America's first combat troops. The soldiers carried their equipment up the sand like World War II heroes. A few months later, after the fighting in the Ia Drang Valley, he photographed stacks of body bags lining the runway at Pleiku.

When my father came back to Hong Kong for Christmas, he couldn't stand the noise of my mother's hair dryer or the electric blender.

'Jesus, Marianne, turn it off!' he shouted. She had to wrap the motor in dishcloths to muffle it. She wanted to make eggnog, the way she always did in New York.

My father carries two cameras. He uses Nikon Fs and Leicas. Extra body armour, he jokes. Once a Viet Cong sniper shot a camera right off his chest. He uses two lenses mostly: a 28mm wide-angle, and a 105mm portrait lens. He keeps rolls of film in specially sewn pockets down the sides of his camouflaged olive-green trousers, where soldiers keep bullets. Two films in his breast pocket, next to his notebook for recording the shots he takes. 'Snaps', he calls them.

~   ~   ~

Frankie makes coffee. We're not supposed to drink coffee and she doesn't know how to make it. It tastes bitter and muddy. We put lots of milk in and drink it anyway, become giddy, excitable, because we're alone and we can do what we like. We're still in our pyjamas. Light cotton Chinese pyjamas with cloth buttons and front pockets embroidered with lotus flowers and pagodas. When Frankie tries to suppress a laugh with her mouth full, she sprays coffee over the table. I grab the newspaper to save it from getting drenched.

There's a story in the paper about a bomb in Wanchai blowing off a policeman's hand: 'a homemade bomb made from firecrackers stuffed in a biscuit tin'. Dozens of bombs have exploded in Hong Kong since the beginning of July. Bombs left in trash cans, on park benches, on the steps to movie theatres. Bombs thrown at policemen or at the British Army patrols which now man the border with China. They are planted by local Red Guards, radical followers of Mao Zedong, who want the British to leave Hong Kong. 'Police urge bystanders to stay away from street demonstrations and to report any suspicious packages,' I read out loud.

There's an update on Tropical Storm Anita, which veered southwest towards Hainan Island at the last moment, merely skirting Hong Kong: 'The colony received an inch of rain last week but the water shortage remains acute. Water rationing will remain in place.' Frankie snorts. It's the rainy season but rainfall's at a record low, the Royal Observatory reports. If you try to turn on the taps, all you hear is a hollow gurgle. A memory of water, like putting a shell to your ear.

'An outbreak of fighting in Canton between Red Guard factions, workers and soldiers from the People's Liberation Army is to blame for a rash of bodies floating up on Hong Kong's shores,' I read to Frankie. 'Horror bodies,' the paper calls them.

'Recent arrivals describe a "state of anarchy" in the provincial capital with bodies lying in the streets, hanging from lampposts, and clogging the Pearl River.' These bodies are carried down the river out to sea.

My mother removes the papers if the pictures are gruesome, the stories violent, but usually she's too late. I study the photograph of Vietnam. I think I see my father.

'He's in the Mekong,' I tell Frankie. 'He's walking down a river lined with trees. There are fish in his trousers. Leeches in his socks.'

'How do you know?' she asks, pulling the paper out of my hand.

four

Frankie's knees scratch against the rattan mat that covers Ah Bing's cot in the tiny amah's room behind the kitchen. She spreads her arms, kneels upon the piece of plywood which serves instead of a mattress, Ah Bing's single blanket neatly rolled up at one end. She rolls her eyes back to show their whites, rocks gently from side to side.

'Ah Bing, the dead person came up right under me, just like this,' she says.

'*Mou chou.*' Be quiet. Ah Bing grunts, and turns away, refusing to look. As if she's afraid the dead woman's spirit might come out of Frankie, float right out of her mouth. Ah Bing's our amah, which means she's our nanny and housekeeper. Or, as she would have it, our Chinese mother.

She squats on a low stool. Her wide bottom engulfs the small wooden seat. Her knees spread to either side like a giant praying mantis. She combs her hair, long, black and thin, down over one shoulder, twists in a false strand to thicken her bun. She has a wide, kind face: strong cheekbones, a flat nose, and generous, long-lobed ears. Good-luck Buddha ears, she calls them. Luck she doubles by wearing a pair of heavy gold earrings which have, over many years, stretched the cartilage. Her face and hands are weathered brown from sun and hard work, but where her black trousers ruck up above her ankles, I can see her skin is as pink and smooth as the inside of a conch shell.

I lie down next to Frankie on the cot, flatten my stomach. I cup my chin in my hands, press my toes against the cool whitewashed wall, watch the smoke from Ah Bing's joss sticks waver in the hot air.

Under her cot, Ah Bing hoards supplies: a pile of my father's worn, faded shirts; jars of dried mushrooms; a pair of my outgrown school shoes, blue and scuffed; a stack of the week's papers to be sold to the *lapsap* woman. Castoffs Mao no longer allows her to send to China even though her relatives write pleading for wool, rice, sugar. The latest regulation: only three catties of new plain-coloured cloth allowed each month. China is proud. It doesn't need second-hand goods. When Ah Bing goes to visit her relatives at Chinese New Year, she wears three pairs of knitted stockings under her trousers to unravel when she gets there. Her punishment is a severe case of prickly rash.

'*Po!* Mao Zedong Dog!' Ah Bing spits. Ah Bing detests Mao. It's because of Mao that her aunt and uncle no longer own their own rice paddies, their own pigs. A cadre of Red Guards, teenagers, no older than Frankie and me, ransacked her uncle's house, smashing everything. The four old elements must be destroyed, Mao said: old customs, old habits, old culture, old thinking. It's the aim of China's Cultural Revolution. Schools are closed, students summoned to be Mao's vanguard. Ah Bing says the villagers were just jealous of her aunt. Her aunt owned more than the others only because she worked harder, and she was smarter.

More hateful is how Mao wrecked the Kuan Yin temple in the middle of the night. Ah Bing narrows her eyes, draws in her breath. Her comb flipping through the air, that's Mao's fist banging on the temple door. Her arm thrust out from her chest is Mao's arm, the many arms of his Red Guards. Like a Tantric Buddha gone mad, they smash the porcelain statuary, rip down the embroidered silk hangings, swing hammers into the carved altar table, shatter the ancient statue of Kuan Yin. Sharp splinters of wood. Buddhism and praying are also forbidden. Religion is backward, 'an opiate of the people'. '*Aiyah!* Mao come! *Hei-san!*' Wake up! The Buddhist nuns woke each other, eyes wide, in the middle of the night.

'Mao sent the young girls home to marry,' Ah Bing mutters, softer now. 'For the old ones, too late. Who would want them?' She lowers her head. I've seen photographs in the paper of monks denounced by Mao, paraded in long robes, hands tied behind their backs, heads bent, their bodies weighed down by huge placards denouncing their backward thinking, their feudal tendencies. Jeering crowds throw vegetables and buckets of human night soil.

'But Ah Bing,' Frankie protests, her tone impatient. We've heard Ah Bing's story before. 'How did Mao make the body float up from the sea?'

'*Po!* Nobody like Mao!' Ah Bing retorts. 'Now everybody tries to swim to Hong Kong. Some, shark eat! Some drown!' Her hands retreat to her hair, which she twists fiercely, netting her braids into a high bun. I want to tell her what I read in the paper about the horror bodies, the fighting in Canton between Red Guards and the PLA. But I can tell she's had enough. Tucked tightly against her temple is a long brass pin with a tiny spoon at one end, which she inserts first in one ear, then the other, gently scooping out the wax. She flicks it clean. Clean of Mao, of China, of us too, insolent *gwaimui*, white ghost girls. Then jabs the pin through her bun.

A pillar of ash tumbles off one of the joss sticks before her small altar to Kuan Yin and down into a Campbell's Soup tin filled with sand. A dank, earthy, wet smell from yesterday's leaf fire seeps in under the edges of a metal-framed door that leads to the back patio, mixes with the other smells of Ah Bing's room: sweet joss, sharp tiger balm, musty clove hair oil, steamed rice. It's bad luck to imitate a dead person. That's why she turns away. Ah Bing knows we're no longer safe. From Mao. From dead bodies. From ourselves. We're changing too fast. We can't be trusted.

Oh Merciful Kuan Yin, she prays, protect me from hungry ghosts. From bodies floating up from the sea. From the foolish pleasure of heathen *gwaimui*. From Frankie *gajie*, older sister. Her bosoms tumbling out of her pyjama top because she isn't careful to button it up. From Katie-ah, *muimui*, younger sister, just beginning to change.

I will shed my skin, Ah Bing says, like a seed breaking from a pod, a snake slithering from its skin, a silk moth chewing its way impatiently out of its precious spun cocoon. Only the lucky survive. Silk-workers throw bags of cocoons into boiling water. The dead worms rattle inside.

In poorly lit factories in southern China, young girls poke the floating cocoons down into the water with forked sticks, turning them, submerging them, waiting for the silk to unravel in the steam. Thread so fine you can hardly see it.

five

Here's a photo of Frankie and me, one my mother keeps on her dressing table. In it, we're wearing light cotton dresses with sashes that tie around the back. The dresses look too young for us, too innocent. They contradict our faces and bodies. They are dresses my mother makes us wear. If you could see our backs, the bows would be crumpled, half-undone, creased with sweat from the hot drive.

Our hair is tidy because my mother asked us to keep the window up. 'The wind will tangle your hair. I want you looking neat,' she said. 'Just for the morning.' If Frankie's braids are tied with ribbons, it's because my mother chose them. Frankie ties them sullenly without bows. She doesn't wear the short, cotton gloves my mother asked Ah Bing to iron for us.

I put the gloves on. It seems so important to my mother. When I inch my scratched, nail-bitten hands down into the gloves, I feel I'm pulling on someone else's skin, whiter, smoother than my own. The skin my mother wants for me. Skin with straight seams that catch when I rub my fingers against one another. The skin I might have, maybe, if I were a real American girl, if we still lived in New York or on my father's farm in Vermont.

~   ~   ~

It's rare, this photo of us. My father photographs the war. He tacks his photographs up on the walls of his darkroom, a former laundry room. A soldier shoots through the open door of a Huey. '*Squirrel hunting*', my father's scribbled underneath. A tall, sad-faced Marine lifts an old Vietnamese woman from the rubble of a burned-out house. The woman's arms stick out stiffly, as if she's scared of being touched. '*Saving Tuyet Diem*', my father's written. A tangled hunk of metal abandoned in the jungle: *French tank at Gio Linh*. A baby's face covered in flies; a mother doesn't brush them away because she's holding her hands out to beg: *Outside Saigon Cathedral*.

There are other photos, labelled simply with place-names: *Chu Lai, Binh Long, Khe Sanh*. Photos of dead bodies, headless, armless, legless, mangled, clothes torn. A pair of delicate, bare feet point outward like a dancer's.

My mother paints landscapes: quiet watercolours of Hong Kong. My mother took the photo of us. My father doesn't go to church. She brought one of my father's cameras with her, one he left behind in Hong Kong to be fixed. Maybe she realized it was a rare chance to present us almost the way she would want us to look. Usually, we go half-naked and barefoot or in flip-flops. But in the picture, we're dressed for church. You can see the arched entrance in the background, the pale yellow of St John's. Next to it, the tapered, grey trunk of a royal palm. Its bark, wrinkled like elephant skin, makes you want to run your hands along it, bare hands.

It's a testament to my mother's strength of will that she gets us to church in this heat. The power of her sudden need to rein us in, dress us, render us up for God's inspection.

~   ~   ~

In the photo, Frankie looks sultry, as sultry as you can in a white cotton dress with puffy sleeves and a bow around the back. You can tell, just from looking at her, these are not the clothes she would choose, this is not the photograph she would take. She'd rather take one of herself naked, sitting cross-legged, eating pomelo in the garden. Her hair would be loose. She'd stare out from under it as from under a veil. She'd rather pose this way — Gauguin's Tahitian native.

Me, I am thin and angular, boyish. My dress hangs off me. My hair is cropped. I look directly at the camera, guarded, slightly hostile. It's an anxious place for me, caught between my mother's need to dress up, maintain appearances, Frankie's desire to strip, to expose herself and everyone else's nakedness.

~　　~　　~

The picture I keep of myself is one my father took in the half-light of early morning. It's underexposed, grey tones instead of black and white. I stick it on the wall next to my bed. You can hardly make me out but you can feel the warm wet, a slight wind. You can smell Ah Bing's steamed rice, her joss, the rotting damp of the garden, hear fishermen heading in, hurrying now because of the typhoon. My face is shaded. Already, you can see I'm quiet, secretive. I keep myself camouflaged.

six

It's Sunday and we're on our way to church.

'Can't we go out on the junk? Can't I stay here with Ah Bing?' Frankie pleads. It's no use. My mother has decided we need God's help.

Dressed, combed, we squeeze into the hot olive-green Morris, a car my father has nicknamed The Pickle. I rest my feet on a gas can we keep full of water for when the car overheats, separate my legs to stop them from sticking together.

'When I was little, your grandmother took me to church every Sunday,' my mother says, encouragingly. 'I had to sit still for hours while she used a hot iron to put my hair in ringlets.' My grandfather was a minister. When my mother was little, she had to call him Reverend or 'Father', never Dad.

Below Pok Fu Lam Road, the sea blinks invitingly. The red flowers of flame of the forest trees burst like firecrackers. Cars full of bathers, picnickers, pass in the opposite direction, heading for Deep Water Bay, Repulse Bay, Middle Bay and Stanley, the string of beaches that line the south side of Hong Kong.

Inside the car, the air-conditioning barely moves the stale air. When I lean forward, my back and arms peel off the vinyl seat.

At Bonham Road, we veer inland under the dark shade of banyans where tangled aerial roots drip down like the beards of old men. Past the Italianate red-brick buildings of Hong Kong University. Shops with roll-up metal fronts and signs painted with red Chinese characters sell soda, film, medicinal herbs, funeral paper. There's a line of idling cars; my mother slows, stops.

'Kate, roll up your window!' she orders sharply. It's a tiny crack, I didn't think she'd noticed, just enough to stick the tips of my fingers out, my white gloves shed on my lap. Three policemen overtake on motorcycles, then three others speed past the opposite way and I realize she's not worried about keeping neat. In front of us, we hear chanting, drumming approaching.

'Red Guards,' Frankie hisses. She peers out, her face flattened against the window. It was worth coming after all. I crane my neck until I too see the marchers approaching down each side of the road.

'Don't look at them!' my mother says. 'Don't make eye contact.' Frankie and I stare. The protesters are young, orderly. Smooth-faced university students with glasses. They wear green caps with the red star of Communist China, wave large red flags crisply, hold up their Little Red Books of Mao's quotations. They look earnest, a little frightened. Some of the girls cling together, awkward and prim like regular schoolgirls. These are not the bomb-throwing leftists, the dastardly Communists we read about in the paper.

'Look, it's him!' Frankie cries, suddenly pointing to my side of the car. A huge mouth with full lips fills my window, kisses the glass, then pulls back.

It's Mao's face, enormous, his broad forehead, hair neatly parted to one side, his lips, the mole on his chin, his high, starched collar, all instantly recognizable. The same picture that's in his Little Red Book, enlarged to poster-size.

'Good thing Ah Bing's not here,' Frankie says.

I look up into Mao's eyes. The eyes of the man who smashed the Kuan Yin Buddha, turned the old women from the temple, sent the dead body floating up under our junk. Mao's eyes are wet and baggy. They look sad and full of longing.

Behind Mao, the students carry other posters, of Marx, Lenin, Stalin, each taller than our car – godlike.

~   ~   ~

My father has told us about Mao. The year of the Long March, when Mao and 80,000 other Communists secretly abandoned their encircled Soviet stronghold in Jiangxi Province. Slipping past Nationalist lines, they forded rivers, climbed mountains and trekked 6,000 miles up into Sichuan and Tibet.

He lies on the floor of our bedroom at night. He bends his knees to keep his back flat because he hurt it in a helicopter crash. Sometimes he has to wear a brace. In the dark, I trace the outline of his body against the black, lacquered floorboards.

'The famous capture of the Luding Bridge, high over the Datong River,' my father begins. 'The Guomindang removed all the wood planks to stop the Communists from crossing. But by night, twenty soldiers managed to crawl, hand-over-hand, across the bare suspension chain. Imagine the river rushing hungrily far beneath them, swirling around jagged rocks and pointed trees. They carried grenades on their belts and in their mouths.'

Maybe that's what makes Mao sad. Remembering the more heroic, simpler days, before his followers rampaged through the streets of China, smashing Buddhist statues, wrecking village homes, setting off bombs in Hong Kong; before he unleashed the Cultural Revolution; before he was old. In those days, Mao never dressed in a starched shirt with a pinching collar. His hair was wild and shaggy, not combed high off his forehead, neatly parted to one side.

Or maybe Mao is remembering his malarial sweats in the freezing cold of the Great Snow Mountain ranges, 16,000 feet high. 'Many of his followers lost their lives or limbs to the cold while Mao's fever burned,' my father continues. 'By the time they reached Yanan, ninety per cent of his troops had deserted or died.'

~   ~   ~

My father tells us bedtime stories of Mao, of Ho Chi Minh, of General Giap, the brilliant commander of the Vietnamese who beat the French at Dien Bien Phu. Of Claire Lee Chennault and the Flying Tigers, a daring band of American pilots who helped the Chinese fight Japan in World War II. He tells us stories of Genghis Khan, the Mongol emperor. And Marco Polo, the great Venetian explorer who travelled the famed Silk Road to China.

He tells us these stories. But he doesn't say how he hurt his back. A crash at Phu Bai, I overheard him tell Lewis, a friend who works for the State Department in Saigon. Viet Cong bullets came right up through the floor past his feet, made the helicopter fall and spin. Phu Bai had been a French base, my father reminded Lewis.

I ask my father what he thought of when his helicopter was hit. Did he think he was going to die?

'I thought of your mother,' he said. 'I thought of the first time she came to visit the farm in Vermont. She was sitting on the porch swing. She was wearing sandals and eating a crab sandwich.'

Seven

'Let us pray in the words our Father taught us.' There is a shuffling, coughing, as worshippers slip from wicker benches to kneel. Following my mother's example, I mouth the Our Father. *On earth as it is in heaven. Lead us not into temptation but deliver us from evil.*

When my mother prays, she clasps the pew in front, buries her face deep in the back of her hands, eyes closed. Next to her, I kneel, upright, awkward, self-conscious. I'm embarrassed by my mother's submission, her humility almost too full, too sweet. Our Father is as foreign to me as Kuan Yin. More so because he doesn't sit familiarly on Ah Bing's bedroom dresser, partaking hungrily of our pyramidal offerings of oranges and lychees. He won't be bribed by prayers of joss and gifts of wrapped candies.

On the far side of my mother, Frankie ducks her head and winks at me. It doesn't bother her that she can't pray. She's a fully-fledged heathen. She'd rather be diving off the junk right now. She won't kneel because it hurts her knees.

I turn away, look up into the high-beamed ceiling, painted blue, where wooden fans drop down from the ends of long, slender poles, spin and shudder like boat propellers. It's like looking up through water.

St John's Cathedral is cool and serene after the hot car ride. Its cane pews, delicate and pretty. Green sunlight, filtered through palms, orchids, bamboo, banyans, streams in through tall arched shutters. From inside, you can hear the muffled whine of work trucks, shifting into low gear as they ascend Garden Road from the Central Business District. Through an open window, I see a flash of a white cockatoo flying up to the Botanical Gardens, a Victorian arboretum and zoo set into the hillside above.

Up in the transept, a stained-glass window shows Jesus standing tall in a storm-tossed boat on the Sea of Galilee. His disciples cower beneath him. Jesus looks sad, I think, like Mao. It will take a miracle to make them believe.

On either side, two smaller windows form a triptych honouring British and Chinese sailors who died during World War II. In one, a British seaman stands to attention before a merchant steamer and a navy gunboat. In the other, a Chinese fisherwoman stands barefoot, two junks sail behind. The fisherwoman's sleeves are rolled up. In her hands, she holds a net. Her bare feet spread warm into the hot, gritty sand.

Frankie wiggles her tongue from side to side, lolls it out of one side of her mouth, rolls her eyes back into their sockets so you can see only the whites. I frown, scared the minister will see her. The congregation's small. We huddle in groups of twos and threes, occupying only a fraction of the pews.

What does my mother pray for? For the body drowned in the sea? To keep my father safe from Viet Cong? Does she pray for us, for the souls of her heathen children? To keep us safe from Mao, Red Guards? To make us more god-fearing, more obedient? Stop us changing so fast? To stop Frankie's antics?

In the church vestibule, there's an old photograph. It shows men in pressed white suits and pith helmets convening for prayer in a mat shed on the Royal Parade Ground. Behind them, grand Victorian buildings and wooden godowns line the waterfront, testifying to the fact that the China traders built their headquarters and safely stored their opium before stopping to build a church.

Hats, umbrellas, tight bodices, laced-up boots, sedan chairs, verandas, potted palms, exotic birds in rattan cages, English voices, cool drinks, silent servants: St John's belongs to the Hong Kong of old photographs, China trade paintings. I feel my mother wrap herself in it, the charm and comforts of the colonial era. She seeks it out when she needs to, reassures herself with its authority, its restrictions, its firm distinction between East and West. A throwback to her father's discipline. It's what draws her here as well as God.

'Hong Kong is facing sinister times,' the minister's voice resounds as we whisper amens, rise up from our knees. Frankie giggles. He is a large and red-faced Welshman with a black beard that prickles the side of your face if you let him embrace you.

'Businesses have pulled out. People have left. Sometimes we feel like Daniel, a small colony, a mere pimple on the mighty continent, standing up against the Babylonian force of China.'

At the word pimple, Frankie snickers. I feel her look my way, drawing out her audience, her prey, her devotee. My mother furrows her brow slightly. She hears Frankie but won't respond.

'Despite the heroic restraint of our police, there has been violence, even death.'

I'm already flustered, trying my best not to notice Frankie's increasingly contorted face, when the minister's sermon is interrupted by the whoop of distant gibbons.

Up close to their cage at the Botanical Gardens, the gibbons' call is deafening. In the church, their cries reverberate louder and louder, low booming howls that accelerate into high-pitched shrieks. *Whooop. Whoooop. Whooooop. Ach-ach-ach-ach-ach-ach.* I can almost see the sleek black monkeys, stretching their long nimble arms from rope to rope, swinging across their cage, air sacs swelling huge under black fur.

The minister forges on though his face beats even redder than before. His complexion makes him look like the posters of Chinese guardians pasted on the doors of temples, the ones with bulging eyes, whiskery faces, who carry long spears and hatchets.

I look to my mother and then I'm caught. For while my mother remains still, politely facing forward, attentive, willing to pretend, believe even that the monkeys don't exist, Frankie stares straight at me. Grinning wildly, she locks me with her gaze, raises her elbow to scratch her armpit monkey-style.

Up in the gardens next to the gibbons is a smaller, grubbier cage housing a troupe of oversexed, blue-bottomed baboons. Each time we visit, they are invariably mating, the male's pelvis thrusting with astonishing, relentless speed, his small hands clutching the female's fur. Now, when Frankie jerks her head up and down, eyes popping, I see at once what she's mimicking. I stare at her, transfixed. Visions of Jesus, Mao, Ho Chi Minh spin in my head. She purses her lips.

Dear God, I pray at last. Don't let Frankie whoop. Please don't let Frankie whoop. But it's too late. Frankie joins the chorus of gibbons. Her whoops, whisper-like at first, inaudible, then louder, full-throated. Whipping around, my mother grabs Frankie by her upper arm and marches us out. Women stare, turn around. I feel the eyes of someone I recognize. Down the cool, tiled aisle, Frankie's body is stiff, resistant, like a convict, as my mother pushes her ahead. The minister momentarily silenced. Through the big wooden doors.

Outside, where no one can see, my mother, rigid, shaking, slaps Frankie hard across the face. Frankie, still a monkey, whoops one last time, then spits.

Dear God, dear Kuan Yin, don't let my mother cry.

~   ~   ~

'It's not Frankie's fault. It was the monkeys. I don't think many people heard her over their noise.' I try to console my mother, make amends.

It's hard for her here, all alone, far away from home, without my father. It's all right for us. It's what we're used to now, the heat, the jungle, the loneliness. I wish I could help my mother. I wish we could be the way she wants us.

eight

The Chinese boy is deaf. His name is Fish. He sits at the edge of the pool, across from me, drawing his feet through the water. His feet are thin and brown. He has long toes, pronounced bones.

We know the deaf boy from school. He's in Frankie's class and is one of the few Chinese students. He has a special tutor who comes each day to help him with his speech and lip-reading. She's from Aberdeen, in Scotland, and has long, red hair and wears earrings and necklaces, unlike the other teachers.

Down at the end of the garden our mothers chat under the shade of a pink awning – Miss Tipley's Sunday lunch party. A pressed white cloth covers the long table; pink, orange, yellow paper-like ranunculi float in glass bowls; blue-and-white china place-settings, glinting silver, pale green wineglasses.

'Miss Tipley's *mo daofu*,' Frankie spouts, surfacing from the water like a whale. Ah Bing told us that word, grinding tofu. 'Miss Innis's her lover.' Grinning, she sinks down again, exhaling a stream of bubbles.

Miss Tipley's a China scholar, a local figure; 'a relic', my father calls her, although she giggles girlishly when he photographs her. I imagine them: Miss Tipley with her grey hair, dishevelled clothes, the loud presumptuousness of her well-schooled English voice, kissing the reserved, much younger Miss Innis. Would Miss Innis take off her thick glasses, whisper to the older, more experienced woman? Would she let Miss Tipley's face draw close to hers, dissolve in a blur?

The deaf boy's toes, trickling back and forth through the cool water, make my face grow hot. It's as if Frankie's words taint me, expose me, allow his toes to caress me, brush my lips. I feel him look at me. He will ask, are you *mo daofu* or would you like to touch me? I pull the towel around my shoulders, look down into the water.

The deaf boy laughs. He says he knows about Miss Tipley. His mother knew her when she was a girl in Shanghai. She called Miss Tipley 'Uncle'. The Chinese were very open about it. He says Penelope always lived like a man, independent, self-sufficient.

The deaf boy calls Miss Tipley and Miss Innis by their first names, Penelope and Jane, something our mother doesn't let us do. The titles Miss, Mrs, Mr, draw a boundary between them and us, mark us safely as children. The deaf boy's mother insists we call her Jen, although our mother would prefer us to say Mrs Tse.

'Come on, then, if you know everything,' Frankie taunts. Hoisting herself up over the edge of the pool, she stands behind him, dripping. She has to wait for him to remove the microphones from his ears and unhook a small, boxy amplifier that hangs around his neck. She grabs his shoulders so that he can't get away, slaps her wet chest against his bare back and shoves. 'Save me, Kate,' the deaf boy pleads before they both tumble over the side. In the water, he's smooth and sleek as an otter and, it surprises me, he's faster than Frankie.

The deaf boy can take us on: two American girls who stake out the pool like sirens. Maybe because he's deaf, he won't have to lash himself to the mast to avoid our cries. He's strong even though he's thin, unbalanced. His bones stick out. Even though he has to speak slowly and carefully to make us understand the slur of his words. His voice warbles as if it's coming through water.

English voices cascade across the garden, loud, commanding, authoritative. The wife of the Chancellor of Hong Kong University is here, as well as the wife of the taipan of Jardine Matheson, one of the oldest China trade companies. She's the woman I recognized in church. We were introduced before we escaped to the pool. Jen and our mother are the only non-English. Ours, the daughter of a prohibitionist New Jersey minister. His, the daughter of a wealthy Shanghai businessman. If Miss Tipley's *mo daofu*, that's why my mother responds so tartly when we ask why Miss Innis lives with her. 'Miss Innis is a secretary,' my mother says.

Miss Tipley's house, her garden, her pool perch at the top of the world like a bird's nest high in the jungle of the Peak. Hong Kong throbs beneath us. Its packed apartment blocks, its busy harbour streaked with boats and white wakes, are framed by a balustrade dotted with potted pink coral plants. And across the water, Kowloon with its quarried hills, planes landing regularly on the runways at Kai Tak. Ferns and St John's lily drip down the mould-streaked rocky cliff out of which the flat garden was carved.

I wonder if the deaf boy knows that Chinese were forbidden to live on the Peak before World War II. The English enacted a law to prevent overcrowding and outbreaks of cholera and tuberculosis and other diseases that raged in the Chinese city. But also to protect themselves from too intimate contact with his race. Miss Tipley showed me photographs of Chinese sedan-chair bearers carrying English men and women up and down the steep slope. Even after the Peak Tram cable car was built, coolies, forbidden to ride it, struggled up slippery, wet tracks carrying loads of ice, coal and food. The colonials sat like gods on Mount Olympus. In winter, these houses literally disappear in shrouds of mist and cloud; their walls streak with wet, their books and clothes rot with mould. I wonder if the deaf boy thinks of these things.

Miss Tipley laughs loudly across the garden, a voice that commands as fluently in Mandarin as in Cantonese. Miss Tipley's Zeus, not Hera. She invites whom she likes. She doesn't need the title *wife*. In 1949, she was thrown out of Shanghai by the Communists. Foreign scholars, missionaries, traders, teachers, all, she was not the only one sent packing to Hong Kong. Flotsam and jetsam, unwanted, undesired. Even though she'd lived in China for more than a decade. A hundred years earlier, the British forced their way into China, prying open its ports, off-loading their poisonous Indian-grown opium, seizing Hong Kong, Miss Tipley said. Now Mao had thrown them out. We can only peer at China across the watery landscape of fish and duck farms at Lok Ma Chau, or search for it in the hard eyes of Chinese soldiers who man the fenced border in Macau.

The deaf boy swims over to the side of the pool where I sit. Water drips from his hair. I see light brown flecks in the dark of his irises. The bones of his shoulders. His skin.

I am grateful to the deaf boy because he isn't shocked by Frankie's pronouncements. Or with the way she lets the thin, wet cotton of her shirt cling tightly to her dark nipples. He wears the microphones in his ears to help him imbibe the song of sirens. He says they don't do much but at least they let people know he can't hear them. If Frankie wanted to whoop like a monkey, he'd be only too pleased.

'Aren't you coming swimming?' he asks.

'Watch this!' Frankie shouts. She springs a neat back-flip off the diving board. Her waves splash. Her shirt floats up. I jump in after. Underwater, I close my eyes. I try to imagine how the deaf boy hears. Sounds are muffled and faraway. The deaf boy pains me.

nine

My father sends Frankie and me a photo from Saigon. It doesn't show soldiers or dead bodies. It's a photo of himself, holding up a duck.

The photo was taken just outside my father's Bureau in Saigon. He holds the duck at arm's length for us to see. My father wears a pressed, white, short-sleeved shirt. Civilian clothes. His skin looks dark against the white. The duck is white too. The photo is black and white. He's put it in a green leather frame.

Behind my father, you can see a pillared gate, a nineteenth-century wrought-iron railing topped with angled spikes and loose rolls of barbed wire. Bureau, it's a French word like Bureau de Poste stamped on the brown envelopes he sends. The French built the stately, two-storeyed villa which *Time* magazine now uses; the spikes and barbed wire are American. Inside the gate is a tall tamarind tree. The tree is dark in the photo, dark and comforting like my father's skin.

My father's office is on Han Thuyen Street. *Time* Bureau, 11 Han Thuyen, Saigon. The address is typed out in leather tags attached to his camera cases. It's written on the packages of film my mother sends on to Saigon. From Han Thuyen, he can walk to his room at the Continental Palace Hotel. I trace the route my father takes, run my fingers along the map on the wall of his darkroom. I follow how he turns right at the cathedral, walks halfway down towards the river. It's an old French map so the names are outdated: Rue Latique instead of Han Thuyen; Rue Catinat renamed Tu Do or Freedom Street. The map shows Le Palais Continental, L'Opéra across the square.

My father found the duck at the Chinese market in Cholon. She was packed into a bamboo cage with her brothers, sisters, cousins, uncles, aunts, my father says, all awaiting their fate in Saigon's restaurants. As he walked by, she stuck her head out between the narrow bars, stretched her long neck along the ground and spoke, quite plainly, in English.

She was a famed courtesan of the Nguyen dynasty, she said, who was turned into a duck by a jealous sorceress. The Nguyen emperors ruled Vietnam for four hundred years before the French and Americans came.

Thach, the magazine's Vietnamese stringer, says my father paid three times too much. He had allowed himself to be swindled by a Chinese, proved himself another guileless *ngu'ò'i Mỹ*, American. The duck isn't fit for a soup.

McKenna, my father's bureau chief, kicks her when he gets the chance, but not too hard. She's a convenient diversion, a live creature to swear at, to chase from the room when the editors, sitting on their asses in New York, have skewed McKenna's stories, edited out his most passionate prose, misled the American public once again. Or when the telex has jammed. Or when he's sent my father to photograph the wrong story. 'Sorry, Michael, I know you've just spent two days getting up to Con Thien. I know the convoy was ambushed. But the big story's at Dak To just now. So get the hell down there.' My father names his pet Saigon Duck.

~   ~   ~

I hear my father tell these stories at dinner parties. The sounds of cutlery, glasses clinking, my mother bringing food, talking, laughter, trickle down the hall to Frankie and me as we sit in bed, reading. My father laughs because he's safe, for ten days, which is how long he comes home. Unless there's another major assault and he gets called back early. Sometimes he can't leave because Ton Son Nhut Airport in Saigon is being shelled. Then my mother drives him to Kai Tak every day to check on flights. He paces up and down the veranda, swearing and gesticulating, angry because someone else might get the pictures before he can.

My father comes home for ten days after every six weeks. Sometimes he leaves early. Other times, he just appears. We wake up in the morning and he's there, eating breakfast, smiling impishly, my mother beaming.

~   ~   ~

Inside the office, Saigon Duck likes to sleep on the top of a filing cabinet directly beneath the waft of the ceiling fan. My father describes to us how she takes an ungainly, flapping leap, then ruffles her feathers and looks around coquettishly, hoping no one has seen. It's her favourite place to sleep after the shade of the tamarind tree. The urgent tapping of McKenna's typewriter, the gentle staccato of Thach's Vietnamese, my father's sudden shouts from the closet he uses as a darkroom all seem to have a comforting, soporific effect.

~   ~   ~

I've seen ducks in cages when we go shopping at the market above Central: ducks, chickens, geese, snakes, sometimes more exotic beasts like guinea fowl or pangolin. Red characters inked on bamboo slats list their prices: 50c a catty for a ringed-neck turtle dove, 80c a catty for a box terrapin. If you want a fresh chicken, the butcher will chop off its head for you. Its eyes pop wide. Its blood runs down the alley into the gutter. If you want snake soup, the proprietor will chop one into his wok, a yellow- and black-banded krait. A glass of snake blood makes you hotter, he says. It's good for winter, too strong in the summer.

While Ah Bing haggles, Frankie and I inspect the pangolin, rolled up like a cannonball. Its armoured scales, long claws for digging insects, prehistoric defences, are useless here in the Chinese market. An old woman pushes up against Frankie, babbling, her teeth stained black with tobacco.

'What's she saying?' Frankie asks, as Ah Bing protectively shoves the woman aside.

'Old lady say pangolin soup will make you *hou leng,*' very beautiful, Ah Bing translates. 'All the boys will want to marry you.' She laughs. There are pangolins in the hills of Hong Kong, a few deer too, civet cats, wild boar and monkeys. Most of them have been eaten, captured like this one to sell at the market, cooked in soups that make you healthy or hot or beautiful. Not for Ah Bing, she's a vegetarian. She doesn't eat meat. She doesn't like men either.

~   ~   ~

The deaf boy knows about pangolins. He knows about tiger grass, bamboo, banyan trees with hanging aerial roots that suck moisture out of the wet air itself. He knows about black-eared kites, swifts, barking deer. He can name the plants and birds as we walk around Lugard Road, a jungly path that rings the Peak.

'Well done!' Miss Tipley says. These things matter to her too.

Behind us, our mothers follow, quietly talking about school, the summer heat.

'When will your husband next be home?' Jen asks. My mother's hair is pinned back. She wears a sleeveless dress, pink and cool, the colour of a flamingo. The deaf boy is thin, gangly. He carries a battered pair of binoculars around his neck.

Miss Tipley says the cockatoos that fly up to the Peak, past her swimming pool, are feral. They're descendants of two pairs released by Major-General Maltby during the war. On Christmas Day 1941, the British commander stepped out along the wide, shady veranda of Victoria Barracks and defiantly released the birds from his aviary. I imagine them, green and red parrots, blue-throated bee eaters, yellow warblers, emerald doves flying out, one by one. Finally, the cockatoos, skimming the tops of the cotton trees like white flags of surrender as the Japanese marched up the road to take Hong Kong.

'He was just selfish,' Frankie says. 'He didn't want the Japanese to get them.'

'That's true,' Miss Tipley agrees. 'Many English burned their furniture and books rather than leave them to the Japanese soldiers.'

The Japanese threw the British and Americans into a prison camp at Stanley village, Miss Tipley says. They tortured and executed many Chinese. Others fled to mainland China because there was so little food in Hong Kong.

The people who stayed had to eat pangolin, cockatoo, snake, monkey, rat, cockroach – whatever they could catch.

ten

Usually my father sends us tapes, wrapped in brown paper. We smuggle them up into the jungle behind the house, away from my mother, from Ah Bing, from Ah Fu, the gardener, who grumbles at us, strange foreign vermin infesting Chinese soil. Past Mr Mok who shuffles out in boxer shorts and an undershirt, carrying a small dish of bugs. He picks the choicest out with chopsticks to feed to a pet mynah bird in a rattan cage. Tufts of black hair sprout from his armpits. Sometimes he spoils the bird with treats. Other times, when it screeches too loudly, he swears and throws a greasy towel over its cage.

Beyond the peeling red railing at the back of the garden, the ground is littered with broken flower pots and discarded roof tiles. A rattan basket collapses towards the ground. A derelict washing machine is half-buried in dirt. We push through palms, past a grove of green bamboo, crawl under the wide translucent leaves of elephant ears. We're American soldiers. Viet Cong. Our feet slip on the rot and mould at the bottom of an old cement nullah, part of a Victorian water-catchment system. Butterflies flit past, tiny yellows, blue-spotted crows. A lumpy toad jumps out of our way.

Three hundred feet up, we scramble on to a cement platform, scratching our knees. It's the ruined foundation of a small house.

'Password?' Frankie asks.

'Ho Chi Minh,' I reply.

The house isn't bombed, just abandoned. Its iron supports stick out rusted and bent, tangled with vines, its stones clasped by roots as the jungle creeps forward to reclaim it, like crashed airplanes or ancient temples sprouting trees.

It's our hideout, a no-man's-land, a place no one will find us, where we keep secret treasures. In Vietnam, girls our age collect shrapnel or nails stolen from USAID projects, deliver them to Viet Cong cadres who pack them into explosives. Our own treasures are more innocent: forbidden chewing-gum begged from the *taitais*, the elderly wives of Mr Mok's father; silk scarves from the Chinese Emporium; cigarettes Frankie pocketed from the purse of a dinner guest.

Most essential is the chunky black tape player our father gave us, a bundle of his tapes neatly bound together with rubber bands, small pieces of him we claim for ourselves. We hide them in a large rusty tin with the words Danish Butter Cookies half scratched off, pushed under a rusted piece of tin roofing.

When we squat, sweaty, our ankles caked with mud, our faces gritty with fern dust, sticky with spider web, we're crouching over a fire that won't burn because the jungle's too wet. My father says the floor of the jungle in Vietnam is so rich with rotting vegetation that it glows at night like phosphorescence in the sea. Bright enough to adjust the settings on your camera, to scribble in your notebook. He says the jungle breathes in and out like a tiger, crouching.

~ ~ ~

Frankie lays out the coloured scarves, lights the stub of a cigarette, passes it to me. I inhale, careful not to breathe too deeply. I'll start coughing because of my asthma. The smoke makes me light-headed. I unwrap the small brown package my father's sent, careful not to rip the stamps, and pass the tape to Frankie who takes charge of the player.

'Hello, children.' My father's voice, alive, deep, crackly, spreads under the green jungle. We hear water running, the sound of a duck quacking. I think I hear my father kick the water from the tap to elicit more sound effects. 'You remember Saigon Duck?' It's hard for my father to begin. Sometimes, he'll rewind the tape several times to get the right start. Saigon Duck's his ruse, his foil.

'Yesterday, I went for drinks with McKenna at the Cercle Sportif,' he says. 'It was warm as usual, but with that heavenly river breeze Saigon gets in the evening. We were just opening a bottle of Algerian wine when there was a noisy commotion at the other end of the patio. At first we thought there might be a fight, or maybe some sort of bomb scare, but then we saw it was just the gardener trying to chase some ducks out of the swimming pool.

'Poor man, he had a rough time of it. Each time he chased the ducks out from one end, they flew back down to the other. They were very noisy and disgruntled. Finally they took offence and flew away, like outraged dinner guests. Later, I realized we don't have a pond at the office and Saigon Duck was probably dying for a swim so I've brought her back to my room at the Continental and put her in the bathtub! It's a very large, old-fashioned tub.'

Saigon Duck's a magic duck, enchanted. A feathered Scheherazade spinning stories to postpone the day her head will be chopped off. In his tapes, my father translates her stories. Stories of a Nguyen princess who falls in love with a fisherman; a loyal queen rewarded in heaven; two courtesans so vain that a goddess turns them into butterflies. 'Exquisite butterflies with shimmering deep-blue wings and tails that drip like teardrops.' My father describes the slow, melancholy way they flap their wings. 'Beautiful for ever but cut off from human love.'

He translates stories of Saigon Duck's later life, digging for bugs and worms along the paddy dykes before she was brought to market. 'She was kept quite comfortably by a well-to-do farmer in the coastal valley near Quang Ngai. A thin strip of arable land nestled between the sea and the blue mountains of the Annamite Cordillera. Green as a parrot's wing.' In the evening, the farmer's daughter would herd her home along the dykes of the paddy fields, my father says. 'Imagine them like black paper cutouts, the line of ducks, the girl with her long willow herding stick, silhouetted against the orange sun setting in the rice paddies.' When he comes home, my father tacks the girl's photograph up on the darkroom wall. *Girl near Quang Ngai*, he scribbles underneath.

Saigon Duck asks my father to describes for us the great stone Buddhas she visited as a child, carved deep in caves of the Marble Mountains, 'near a place called Danang'.

'There are five outcrops of rock that make up the Marble Mountains. Each one is named after a different element: water, fire, metal, earth, wood. They jut up unexpectedly, like the drip castles we sometimes make together on the beach. Twisted, hollowed by wind and rain. The Vietnamese believe they are the remnants of a giant turtle egg.

'Saigon Duck wants me to tell you how the Buddhas are lit from above by an other-worldly green-blue, sunlight refracted as it seeps through cracks and fissures in the earth. I would like to visit them one day.'

As I listen to my father's voice, I imagine the great Buddhas, green and blue as if they were underwater. I feel I am swimming in to see them. Butterflies whirl around me. Ducks dive from above, snatching at fish.

'He never tells us anything,' Frankie interrupts. She lies hunched over the tape player watching the cassette spool round, like a cat eyeing its prey. Her shoulders are brown, strong, ready to spring. Her dark hair spreads loose along the pink, orange, blue of the scarves.

'Maybe Saigon Duck doesn't know about the war,' I say stupidly. 'Maybe she doesn't read the newspaper.'

Frankie laughs. She sits up, relights the stub of her cigarette as if she hardly cares to listen to the rest. When she breathes out, the smoke curls from her nose like a dragon.

She's right, of course. We've read about the fighting along the Central Coast, about the American bombing campaigns in Quang Ngai and Quang Tin. We know about Viet Cong mortar attacks on the Danang airstrip. In our Danish Butter Cookie tin, we keep a handful of photographs we've lifted from the darkroom bin, slightly crumpled, discarded because they are blurry or badly exposed. One, marked Quang Ngai, shows a thirty-foot palm tree blown right out of the ground into a nearby rice paddy. In another, taken from the air, some families cook over a fire at the black entrance to an underground tunnel. The charred remains of villages make ugly, grey squares in the lush landscape.

Saigon Duck's stories are fairy tales for children. In them we don't grow up. We have to ferret out the stories my father doesn't tell, fill in the relevant facts, the things we need to know, like hunter-gatherers, enemy spies. The reason he can't visit the Buddhas is that the Viet Cong hide there. It's from those outcrops, the jagged shell of a turtle's egg, they rocket Danang. Night explosions shake the Marine press camp along the Han River where my father stays.

Late at night, travelling opera troupes sent from Hanoi sing anti-American ballads. Their high voices echo through the caves, lifting the spirits of the Viet Cong, filling them with ardour. Towering above, the Buddhas look down, huge, serene, indifferent.

~   ~   ~

I clasp my hands around my knees. Bury my eyes, pressing them into the dark of my bones. Listen to the noises of Pok Fu Lam village drifting up: a dog barking, a radio whining, the distant throb of a jackhammer, calls of workmen. The chatter of crested bulbuls, noisy birds that flit from tree to tree. Sailing into Hong Kong, a pair of junks from China, their red-brown sails patched like the mended shirts under Ah Bing's bed. The junks bring pigs and ducks. Sometimes they smuggle refugees who hide in their airless holds, knee-deep in bilge water, waiting to be dropped off on outlying islands. There are people who drown trying to swim across to Hong Kong, the bodies Ah Bing spoke of. Other bodies float down the Pearl River, from the fighting in Canton.

I try to imagine my father's room in Saigon. It's big and dark. A mosquito net is tied over the bed. There's a map on the wall. The chunky child's magnet he borrowed from us, and tweezers, to help pry tiny bits of shrapnel out of his shin. An instruction manual for newly issued infrared, night-vision goggles. His helmet. Otherwise, his room is fairly spartan. Except for his cameras, my father travels lightly, a single suitcase of clothes, his film, a notepad in his front pocket for keeping a record of the photos he takes, the places he's been.

When it rains, he'll throw open the doors to his balcony, let the rain wash the salty sweat from his face, his hands, soak his white shirt. Across the square, he'll look down on the old French Opera House and the modern Hotel Caravelle.

I imagine my father. He's sitting on the closed lid of the toilet seat, his back leaning against the mould-streaked wall, his legs pulled up, feet resting on the chipped porcelain of the bathtub where he watches Saigon Duck preen. The spools of the tape player wind around quietly. Through the shuttered window, the sounds of Saigon cry out: the roar of motorbikes, Hondas and Cambrettas, so loud, it's as if they tear through the room; cyclo drivers offering 'good price' to wary hotel guests; the high, persistent pleas of refugee children begging for money; the scratch of palm fronds against the shutter. The feel of the heat is like here, I think, but carries different smells. The smell of the Mekong, of triple-canopy jungle, of artillery fire. My father's quiet now. He holds the tape player on his knees. It's hard for him to remember us sometimes. He loves Vietnam so much.

eleven

Red banners. Red flags. Little Red Books of Mao Zedong's edicts wave in the air. Red bursts of firecrackers. Red drums. Red Guards. We see them well before the ferry docks: over at the far end of the village, where old men usually sit and play mahjong under the shade of banyan trees.

'Sons of dogs. Whores' children. Troublemakers,' Ah Bing mutters. Too young to know, or care, what Mao has done to China. Her China. What can these people know of her auntie, beaten in her home? *Po!* Even worse for second uncle who could only turn his head. They held him back, tied his arms. Jars of rice wastefully thrown to the floor. Nightdresses, clothes all torn. Auntie's precious necklace scattered. What did the Red Guards want with her auntie? She only had one pig, a small bit of land. She wasn't rich like Hong Kong people. Later, second uncle was found. He had hanged himself from a tree.

'Useless no-goods, stupid, spoiled sons of bitches in heat,' Ah Bing swears. Playing with troubles bigger than they know.

The noise of the protest is momentarily drowned out as the ferry engines are thrown into reverse. '*Mui Wo. Mui Wo*,' a recording blares through the loudspeaker. A shower of nutshells, pits, plastic wrapping, cigarette stubs cascades down over the railings into the white frothy sea. Sailors in blue uniforms throw heavy mooring ropes.

In China, the Red Guards smashed her temple, confiscated the property. Mao stole it, she says. Here on Lantau Island, she and her friends have built a new temple. She likes to bring us along on her day off.

'*Fai di la. Fai di.*' Hurry. Hurry. Ah Bing herds us towards the gangway. Huffs as the upper ramp is lowered first. Why pay an extra fifty cents to sit on the top deck when it's perfectly nice down below? 'Topside is for *gweilos* and rich people,' she says.

When it's our turn, we surge forward, push on to the ramp even before it bangs down on the high concrete pier. Frankie and I elbow and shove. We're as fearless at that as local children. We manoeuvre past fishermen, village women laden with bags, a man wheeling a large object covered with a plastic sheet. It's an entire cow's leg; the bloody hoof sticks out, attracting flies. In front of us, a shopkeeper pushes a cart with trays of tofu, white fleshy squares that wobble under a wet cloth. '*Hou sun sin,*' very fresh, Ah Bing croons. She'd like to stop him and buy some but a group of village women push us forward, shouting high-pitched advice.

'*Aiyah.* What's all that commotion up ahead?' they ask. 'What are all those city people doing here?'

On our way up to the temple, Ah Bing will stop to buy some fresh fruit. 'Good sweet mangoes, smooth and yellow,' she says. 'Longans, dry and crinkly like old ladies' skin. But inside, plump and ripe like the flesh of young girls.'

'*Aiyah*, much too dear,' her sisters at the temple will protest. 'You take them home. Give them to Katie and Frankie, ah.' But of course they expect these gifts. Their protesting's just a game, like the way they pretend it's good times again back in China. Try to forget what's happened. Families without enough rice.

And later, they'll eat the fruit, but only after they've left it out on plates – colourful, sweet offerings to Kuan Yin.

Maybe she'll buy Frankie and me some sugar cane. Once when she was young, her uncle bought her a stick of sugar cane, Ah Bing told us. When he sliced back the hard green skin with a big knife, he looked so serious she wasn't sure if he was angry with her or not. She sucked and sucked until all the sugar was gone, worried he might take it away. Her uncle laughed. Her mother laughed.

That was after they had sent her away to another family. Too many girls to feed. But she had come back. She didn't like the other family. She walked home. It took her two days. 'I remember my mother's face when I came back,' Ah Bing said. 'She was so happy to see me.'

The crowd at Mui Wo is like on market days in China, Ah Bing says. A fisherman brushes by; the smell of his brown skin, sea salt and hot sun, fills her nostrils. '*Po!* A man's smell is too strong.' She can't remember the smell of her own father. She was too young when he died.

We cross a narrow bridge over a muddy inlet crushed with sampans. Below us a boat woman squats, mending fishing-nets. A girl balances along the gunnels of two boats tied side to side. She carries a baby brother or sister fastened tightly to her back with a red cloth to ward off bad spirits.

~   ~   ~

Red banners. Red Flags. Red drums call from across the village. The sound of a megaphone blaring.

'Let's run ahead,' Frankie whispers, pulling me close. It's our chance to see the real Red Guards, not the smooth-faced students we saw through the car window. 'Come on,' Frankie persists. 'Ah Bing will never let us go.' *Bang, bang, bang, bang*, a shattering noise bursts around us like machine-gun fire. For an instant, the crowd stops, sucks in air all at once; we hold our breath. The sons of whores have let off a string of firecrackers. Folding my arm into hers, Frankie tugs. We bolt forward, laughing.

~   ~   ~

Tubs of fish slosh at our feet as we hurry past: flabby groupers, blue lobsters, stacks of sand-coloured crabs, their claws bound with straw, left in the hot sun like prisoners of war. At the edge of the cement seawall, a fisherwoman scales and guts a red snapper. Her customer nods appreciatively as the fish flails because it is so fresh. Fish scales and blood fly everywhere.

Stacks of *bok choi*, Chinese cabbage, asparagus beans, spiky jackfruit laid out on giant leaves of elephant ears. Usually, we'll linger by the sugar cane, pester until Ah Bing buys us two sticks. We'll chew them all the way up to the temple, spitting the sucked fibres along the cement path. But today we rush past, dodging imaginary bullets, black umbrellas, blue-and-white flip-flops, red plastic ladles that hang down from stall-fronts like prizes in a fair.

Glancing back, I catch a brief glimpse of Ah Bing, still near the bridge. She stretches up on her toes trying to see where we've gone.

'She'll just think we lost her in the crowd,' Frankie reassures. We know the way up to the temple.

Her children, ah. Where are we? *Po!* She can't see anything. She's too short. She needs to catch up, take us inland along the back of the village, away from the Red Guard trouble.

Come on. Come on. Ah Bing would keep us safe, she'd stop us if she could.

twelve

Amid the noise, the beating of drums, the Red Guards look hot and irritable when we reach them. Their leader, a man in a dark, sweaty suit, looks out of place among the others who wear open work shirts or sleeveless undershirts. He paces up and down, his voice cracking as he exhorts Mao's followers through a tinny megaphone. Up close, the crowd's responses sound worn and tired.

'Throw out Governor Trench!'

'Liberate Hong Kong for Honourable Chairman Mao!' The men are older, rougher-looking than the students we saw near Hong Kong University. Workers brought in from the city, maybe. I've read that the Communists pay people to attend their demonstrations. One or two of them glare at us: two imperialist infiltrators. I'm relieved when Frankie hangs back, pauses next to a vegetable stall.

At the entrance to a narrow alley, a man gapes at us. His face large, pasty and baby-like. The way his mouth hangs open, I notice he's missing a bottom tooth. I turn away, move closer to Frankie.

'Ruffians and agitators,' Frankie whispers, quoting the kind of breathless descriptions we read in the newspaper.

'*Chaiyan! Chaiyan!*' Police! Police!, a small clutch of children call out as they run past, shimmy up a nearby banyan tree.

In front of us, a muscular man in an undershirt grabs the megaphone out of the Communist leader's hands and jumps up on a stone mahjong table. He shouts. His face grows red. The veins on his neck swell and throb. The protesters look past him now towards the ferry pier, crane their necks, rise up on toes. The two bare-chested drummers start to pound their drums more quickly, faster and faster, their bodies glistening with sweat.

Frankie pulls me forward to follow the children. Under the tree is a hunk of rusty metal, an old engine of some sort. We scramble up and now we too can see the trim black-and-white police boat from Hong Kong. It has pulled up behind the ferry and disgorges a neat, orderly line of policemen. There's a distinct edge of fear now within the crowd. Demonstrations are illegal in Hong Kong, as are firecrackers. I wonder if Frankie and I could be arrested; whether Ah Bing could find us if we were, or my mother.

The police look like creatures from another planet, dressed in full riot gear, helmets, shields. They've been issued with special non-slip boots and perspex goggles, batons which can shoot bullets into the knees of attackers. They carry no guns.

'Imperialist tools! Traitors! Running dogs!' the demonstrators taunt now, in high voices, itching for a fight.

Around us, shopkeepers hastily close their stalls, squirrel away their money, pull down awnings, then the metal grates. The old fisherwoman stares open-mouthed, with gold-tipped teeth, at the Communists who have come from nowhere, wraps her fingers around the handles of her small bucket of fish. Merchants scuffle with Red Guards who grab their fruits and vegetables to throw at the police. A group of men fill their pockets with stone and rubble from a building site. Quiet, faceless, the police form a phalanx at the far end of the market.

'We better go!' Frankie yells, jumping down off the engine. She has to shout over the noise of the crowd and the drums. She's grinning, her eyes ablaze. This is the real thing. Something we'll read about in tomorrow's paper. It's what we want, to get close, to see the Red Guards, all the things my father doesn't tell us about Vietnam.

Thirteen

Away from the seafront, a maze of narrow alleys zigzags to the back of the village. Market stalls press in tightly, blocking the bright sunlight, the noise of the demonstration, but they are closed, deserted. The shopkeepers have gone home or hurried to watch the spectacle. The air smells of dried fish, squid and octopus wizened and pressed flat, fresh ginger root, sweet medicinal herbs. Open gutters glisten with dark slime. A red bucket collects drips from a public tap.

'We're going to catch it from Ah Bing,' Frankie says, laughing. Her voice echoes, too loud. We should whisper back here. Keep quiet. I'm anxious to hurry now, through to the open fields where we can find the path to Ah Bing's temple. Maybe we shouldn't have left Ah Bing. Maybe we won't be able to find our way. I follow Frankie, wishing we were already there. Then we stop.

In front of us: a pair of black slippers, baggy black trousers stretch across wide hips, an open shirt reveals a gold necklace marooned on a clammy, white chest. Somehow I know instinctively, before I look up, that it's the man I saw earlier with the pudgy face. His small piggy eyes make me cringe. His pink tongue is thrust into the gap where his tooth is missing. Quickly we turn back. But behind us, a second man steps out from a hidden corner. This man is taller. He has large hands and his face is covered with pockmarks. Frankie screams. But the pockmarked man grabs her quickly around the mouth, silencing her, while the pudgy man pushes me forward, shoves me through the opening of a small metal door.

Inside, it is dark and stiflingly hot. There's a raw, rancid smell. At first, I can't see anything. Thin slats of light that break in around the edges of the tin siding help me find Frankie; to decipher the strange shapes that hang before us: flattened ducks, pigs' trotters, entrails dangling from hooks. We're in a butcher stall. One that closed hastily because the butcher's block is stained with blood and bits of flesh. There is a sharp cleaver, a flat razor, the kind butchers use to scrape the greasy markings off pigskin. The smell is sickening.

'Come now, you don't want any trouble!' the pudgy man says. His voice is low and gravelly in contrast to his baby face. In his fleshy fist, he holds something: a shopping bag of woven plastic mesh. He must have kept it in here. I hadn't noticed it outside. He holds the bag at arm's length as if trying to keep it away from his body.

Behind me, a big shadow; it's like looking at the dark side of the moon. Snickering, the pockmarked man kicks the animal so it sways gently back and forth. A huge pig hanging from a large hook.

'*Hou leng muimui*,' pretty little sister, the pudgy man says. His voice falsely sweet like a kindly uncle, like a boy playing with an insect before he squashes it. 'You don't want to make trouble. Take this bag down to the ferry pier, the police boat. This bag is full of lychees for police captain. Very nice present. Police captain, plenty good friend.

'Don't look inside!' he adds, his voice rough once more. As

if I could see anything in here. He forces the bag into my hand. I pull back, not wanting to touch his skin. 'Maybe next time I'll bring nice lychees for you. *Nei teng?*' You understand?

Frankie squirms, manages a quick gasp before the pock-marked man tightens his grip around her mouth. With his other hand, he presses her wrists together too tightly. The bag is in my hands now. My fingers curl stiffly around the hard plastic handles.

Frankie makes a high, muffled noise from her throat. She doesn't want to be left or maybe she's trying to tell me something, to scream. The big man pulls her arms painfully up her back, shoves her against the tin siding so that her chin pushes upwards and her neck stretches long and white.

'*Jau la!*' Go!, the pudgy man barks. He's angry at Frankie for struggling, causing trouble. 'You no come back, you no big sister!' I look at my sister's neck, the knife on the chopping block. The next thing I know I am pushed out in the sunlight; the bag of lychees dangles from my hands. I choke on fresh air, blink at the light.

~   ~   ~

Where do I go? Back down to the village, to the police boat as I've been told? Or up to the temple? Run! Up to the temple! Find Ah Bing! Get help! Help me, Kuan Yin. But if I go to the temple, the men will see me. They might have spies.

Slowly, quietly, I step towards the sea, the bag of lychees heavy in my hand, too heavy. Heading back along the alley, I feel as if I float through the air without legs, without will. My spirit has left my body, stayed with Frankie. Only the lychees pull me forward.

Silently, I memorize my route: red bucket, sweet medicines, basket of ginger root, dried fish. I recite these markers like a mantra that will lead me back. Don't worry, Frankie. I'll come back. Even though I'm very small. *Gwaimui*, white ghost girl. Even though I'm all alone, not looked after. Ah Bing would look after me if she could.

Wrinkled cucumbers, bruise-coloured eggplants loom huge and out of focus. I hear the Red Guards shouting, threatening the police. Still beating their drums as if nothing's changed, nothing's happened to Frankie and me. I don't look at them. Don't look up. I'm scared. Scared someone will see me, look in my eyes. The eggplants are my last marker, the entrance to the alley. I recite my mantra backwards: purple eggplant, dried fish, basket of ginger root, red bucket, metal door.

Let me be invisible, I pray. Don't let anyone see me. Not the police, not Ah Bing, not my mother, not the deaf boy. Don't let him see me floating in midair, carrying the white flesh of lychees. Two women push a large basket of long beans inside their stall. '*Loi la.*' Come, one says, offering help, protection. I see the wrinkled backs of her hands, her black trousers, the fullness of her basket. I don't look at her face.

Quietly I walk under the children in the banyan tree. Don't look up. I try not to hold the bag too far from my body, the way the pudgy man did, too revealing. It's just fruit. A present for the police captain. I keep close to the stalls for cover.

Around me, the villagers and shopkeepers wait, holding their breath. Who will make the first move? Can't they see me? A white pawn? Moving forwards? Why don't they stop me? There's a buzzing in my ears that drowns out the noise; the blare of police, who issue orders through their own mega-phones, makes it all sound faraway. 'Please co-operate peacefully. Please sit down and let the police escort you peacefully back to Hong Kong.'

It's because I'm good at this. That's why they don't see me, run out and stop me. I've been in training. Hiding out. Playing Viet Cong with Frankie. I'm more subtle than the pudgy man. Camouflage, secrets, deceit, they're second nature. It's because I'm *gwaimui*, white ghost girl. I can make myself invisible, hide behind my white skin. I can dodge rocks that the Red Guards hurl at the police, bullets in the jungle. I can't be hurt. I'm nimble for my age, quick-witted, the Viet Cong say. They use me as a child scout, a lookout. I carry baskets of shrapnel, nails I've stolen from aid projects. I smuggle them through underground tunnels to soldiers who pack them into bombs.

~   ~   ~

Looking up, I see that I can't possibly take the lychees up the pier. The police have cordoned off that whole side of the village. They stand guard at the bridge over the inlet of sampans where a woman mends a net and a girl carries a baby on her back. I won't be able to pass.

I hesitate. I feel a pair of eyes, a police officer's, pick me out. I feel his gaze, his surprise, a small white girl alone in the Chinese market, carrying a shopping bag full of lychees. The police officer picks up a radio receiver. The bag of lychees is huge and grotesque. It pulls at my arm. My clenched hand is sweaty. I edge back behind the side of a fruit stall to escape his view. To hide what I carry.

'No,' I whisper. 'Don't help me. I don't want your help. Don't stop me.' There's an empty oilcan, tall, dented. This is as close as I will get to the police because the pier is cordoned off.

I don't think I can bear the weight of the lychees any more. Quickly, without looking, I drop the bag into the can. Hear the lychees hit the bottom with a horrible clang, the sound of metal striking metal. I'm surprised no one else hears. No one runs out to stop me.

Hurry now, don't run. I walk briskly. I need to get back to Frankie but also instinctively I'm putting space between myself and the lychees. Between myself and the police. It's hard not to run. But if I do, people will know what I did.

The explosion, it's deafening. A huge single blast, like all the firecrackers blown up at once. There's a shout. I hear a boy's high voice scream, without stopping. The police charge forward, shields up. Protesters, villagers, shopkeepers, children scatter, running back into the alleys for safety. No one wants to be arrested. No one wants to be hurt. I see the suited Communist leader standing empty-handed and confused. It's not what he bargained for.

I run fast now, carried, hidden by the crowd. Turn into the alley at the eggplants. Eggplants, dried fish, basket of ginger root, sweet medicines, red plastic bucket, metal door . . . The door is open. Where's Frankie? I throw myself inside, ready to scream at them, tear them to pieces. I couldn't do what you asked. Give me back my sister. What have you made me do?

'They're gone.' Frankie's voice in the dark. She crouches in the corner behind the slaughtered pig, her back up against the hot metal. She is here after all, my sister. She's all right. She's alive. I've done it. I've saved her.

I lean over to pull my sister up, to embrace her, but she pushes my hands away as if they are dirty or maybe she is. She gets up herself.

'You shouldn't have left,' she says, her voice angry and choking. 'You don't know what they could have done.' Outside her eyes are wide and dilated. I'm taken aback, wounded. I thought she would welcome me back, a heroine. Instead she's accusing me. 'What was in the bag?' she asks.

'I didn't look,' I say. 'I threw it in an empty can. Then I came back — I thought they might kill you.'

'There was an explosion,' Frankie says. She looks at me hard. Then dizzy, her vision blurry, she throws up in the gutter.

fourteen

Red embroidered silk. Tassels. Red stubs of joss sticks. A large coil of joss hangs from the ceiling, smoking. Porcelain bowls bear offerings to Kuan Yin: Ah Bing's mangoes, longans, dried mushrooms, sticks of incense wood. Red shakers of fortune sticks. Fortune papers tacked on the wall. Red tablets with gilt lettering. Red plastic pinwheels turn before a grease-caked fan. A red bucket holds a rag, a feather duster, a greasy cooking-oil bottle now used for detergent. A magenta canteen with white peonies steams with jasmine tea.

On the wall, a painting of Kuan Yin. She wears a blue dress, floats across the ocean on a pink water lily.

Frankie is sick again. She threw up in the algae-choked stream on our way up to the temple. The amahs bring her tea and congee to settle the stomach.

'Missee say warm Coke number one,' Ah Doi pushes her own remedy. Ah Mui insists that we turn off the fan. Ah Bing makes Frankie take off her clothes. They smell awful, 'like bad meat'. Frankie pulls a sheet around herself and shoves the clothes through the curtained door of Ah Bing's sleeping cubicle upstairs. She pulls the curtain, shutting out everyone, shutting out me. The small room has an interior window to let in light but the glass is etched, I can't see through.

I help Ah Bing wash Frankie's clothes in a tub on the patio. She doesn't say anything to me either. We wash in silence. I want to cry. When Frankie knelt down on the path to vomit, Ah Bing swore at us. '*Diu ke lo si.*' Make love to your old teacher. '*Houh hoi.*' Little whores. The words soothed me. They were the first words she spoke after the police let us go.

~   ~   ~

Ah Bing waited for us near the ferry pier. She didn't go ahead to the temple. The policeman who found us said he knew who we were because Ah Bing had reported us missing. She'd run up the pier, accosted the entire police force in riot gear. What would she tell the missee if she lost the children? There would be plenty of trouble if we were hurt. And now there'd been a bomb!

'*Nidi neige gwaimui?*' Are these your white ghost children? the police officer asked. I was startled by how small and frightened Ah Bing looked sitting by the side of the pier. She tried to look after us.

'*Aiyah!* Bad girls, naughty girls!' Ah Bing jumped up when she saw us, grinning a mouth of gold teeth. She slapped the police officer familiarly on the arm. '*Gei hou panyau.*' Very good friend.

The officer didn't know what to do. We're only children. We were also the only *gwailos*, whites, except for a group of hippies wearing leather sandals, long skirts and beads, who waited at the pier. And a single British officer, a few yards away, who was barking questions at the handcuffed Communist leader. The Communist was still wearing his dark suit. Two junior officers held him roughly by either arm. One interpreted. The other kicked the back of his knees, making him fall forward.

~   ~   ~

The fruit stall was blown up. We saw it when we walked back to the pier. There was a pool of blood on the cement path. The police boat left, speeding back to Hong Kong.

The officer who found us wanted to question us. The police had seen a white girl like me just before the bomb went off, he said. But Ah Bing intervened, arguing heatedly in Cantonese.

'*Pak tuali.*' Ridiculous, she said, placing her large body strategically between us to ward him off. Our father is a photographer for an American magazine, very rich, very important, she warned.

Hearing the fracas, the British officer glanced our way, then walked over.

'I understand you ran away from your amah,' he chided in a mocking tone. When he placed his thick, white hand on my shoulder, I thought he would arrest me but he only meant to reassure. To him, we were naughty children, like his own maybe. He can't imagine us as witnesses, or criminals.

I felt my body shake. The bag was too heavy. It made a loud clang when it dropped.

'You're both very lucky you didn't get hurt,' the British officer admonished, more earnestly. 'But I can see you've learned a lesson. You better go up to your amah's temple until we've cleaned all this up.' He nodded to the Chinese officer, who backed off reluctantly, then returned to his interrogation of the Communist leader. Didn't he notice how badly Frankie smelled? Didn't he realize what would have happened if I had taken the lychees to the ferry pier?

~   ~   ~

We wring out Frankie's clothes. The water splashes into the tub. My hands are not part of my body. I watch them shake. I feel cold. On top of her sleeping cubicle, behind a red-lacquered railing, Ah Bing keeps a thick wool sweater knitted with leftover yarn and a broken transistor radio my mother threw out. I want to wrap the sweater around me, button the big buttons, thrust my hands into its front pockets, even though the heat swathes me in sweat. I want my father to fix the radio so we can all listen, out on the patio. We could sit cross-legged on the cement, me, my father, Frankie, Ah Bing, Ah Doi, Ah Mui, Ah Kuan. Listen to the BBC World Service. It would tell us what was happening in Vietnam. Report an explosion on Lantau Island.

I wander into the Kuan Yin room and stand before the altar. In the kitchen, the amahs sputter their disapproval, their disgust with Communists, their hatred for Mao; they apportion blame. Outsiders stirring up trouble. And what about us, Ah Bing's *gwaimui* children, who ran off? What blame do we get?

I light three joss sticks; three not four. Four, *sei*, is bad luck because pronounced differently it means death. I bow, three times, as Ah Bing has taught me; then stir the fortune sticks in their bamboo canister. Ah Sun sits in a dim corner folding paper offerings for the dead and piling them up on a square table. She's too old, too blind and too lame to help in the kitchen. Her thick cane leans against the wall.

These women in the temple are Ah Bing's Buddhist family, her 'brothers', 'uncles' and 'nephews'. They look after each other in old age and will worship each other after death, tend each other's ancestor tablets. In this way, they won't become hungry ghosts.

'When I die, Ah Kuan will wear pearl earrings for one year,' Ah Bing boasts. 'She will wear white and cry for me.' Ah Kuan is Ah Bing's 'son'. They met in Singapore before the Japanese invaded, when they were young. Like Ah Bing, Ah Kuan is sturdy and practical. She has a wide, mottled face and blinking eyes like a grouper. She lives at the temple as caretaker. Ah Bing chose her son well. She didn't choose me.

Ancestor tablets line the walls of the Kuan Yin room: small blocks of wood with black-and-white photographs that stare out. One is of a young girl. The expensive blocks have gilt lettering and carved red dragons winding up the sides. Laymen pay the nuns to keep their family's tablets here, to say prayers for them, light offerings. Once, when I reached up to take one down, there was a large cockroach hiding behind it. Ah Doi caught it in her bare hand. The women believe part of the soul resides in these tablets after death.

I shake the sticks, ask Kuan Yin what will happen to me. Will the police come to get me? Will the pudgy man come after me, bring me more lychees? Will Kuan Yin make Frankie better? Will my father come home to look after us? Please come home.

As I shake, one of the fortune sticks forces its way up, hovers tall above the others, falls out on the altar. I read the number, written in Chinese, then go to the wall to find the corresponding fortune. It's printed on a thin piece of cheap, pink paper with red characters that run down in four straight lines. Ah Sun taps her cane against the wall to catch my attention. I bring her my fortune and she smoothes it out on the table next to the folded money for the dead. I wonder if Ah Sun is already thinking about offerings being burned for her, about her photo on an ancestor tablet. Her hands are knotty and mottled with sunspots. She smoothes the paper with the side of bent knuckles and looks at it a long time. She looks up at me, her eyes watery and milky with cataracts. She has high cheekbones and white hair. She mumbles through toothless gums, singing, chanting. It's a high-pitched ballad about my fortune, my life.

The ash on the joss sticks I lit piles up in neat pillars before Kuan Yin. The air is thick with smoke. Moths hang unmoving from the tapestries and the ceiling, drunk on joss. One is bright green. Another is camouflaged to look like a piece of bark. A large white moth spreads furry wings over a stick of incense wood, chewing in a drugged stupor. The amahs say the moths are spirits, that it's something of a miracle how they come. Behind a rich red tapestry, a dark polished Kuan Yin gazes down with lidded eyes. Renouncing the world and seeing it all at once. Her eyebrows arch regally. She knows what I've done.

I listen to Ah Sun's chant rise up into the smoke. As indecipherable to me as the red characters on pink paper, yet soothing somehow, comforting. I will shed my skin like a snake, like a seed from a pod, a silk moth chewing its way impatiently from its precious, spun cocoon, Ah Bing said. And when I spread my wings, I will not be *gwaimui*, white ghost girl, any more. I will be Red Guard, Viet Cong.

I watch the moths. I don't want to think of the market any more. Of the pudgy man, his pasty face. I don't want to think of the lychees, their weight, the police, the cleverness of

Vietnamese girls, a boy screaming, Frankie's words in the dark.

I want the blue dress of Kuan Yin. I want to float across the ocean on a pink lotus. My hair blows in the wind. I am far away. A bird brings me an amulet.

fifteen

In my mother's room, the edges of the newspaper stick out under a pile of books. Heavy books about Miró, Prendergast, Chinese brush painting. If she's hidden the paper, there is bad news she doesn't want me to see.

My mother's up early. It's a water day. She's leaning over the tub filling plastic buckets. Four hours of water every fourth day. Because one storm after another has drawn near the colony, only to veer off at the last minute. Typhoons Violet, Anita, Fran, Iris. I can count them on my fingers, name my mother's plastic buckets after them — miniature pools spreading across the bathroom floor. The city left sweltering in unrelieved heat, pungent, stinking. A hundred degrees already this morning. At Pok Fu Lam Reservoir, we've watched the water level drop, red clay sides exposed like scars beneath banks of lush green jungle.

'Baths tonight,' my mother says without looking up.

I lift the books, pull the paper out. It sags in my hand with the damp. Black ink rubs off on my fingers. My mother could see the smudges if she looked.

LANTAU BOMB OUTRAGE. DASTARDLY ACT BY COMMUNISTS. Words set in bold, heavy print. Inescapable. WOMAN KILLED. BOY BADLY BURNED.

I shove the paper back under the books where my mother put it. If you hide, press the words down heavily enough, you can try to make them go away. You can pretend there is no Vietnam War. Your father is home.

My mother lifts a bucket from the tub. Water sloshes on to the green tiled floor, wetting her bare calves, soaking the ends of a pale cotton skirt she's tucked behind her knees. Her face and neck drip with perspiration. Her muscles strain. She's more beautiful than either Frankie or me.

Mummy, I want to whisper. I didn't know what to do with the lychees of the pudgy man. I saw the market stall ripped apart. There was a pool of blood on the path. I try to speak, to whisper, but the words don't come.

'Kate, go fill the vases in the front patio,' my mother says, still without looking at me. Filling the garden vases is our usual task, one Frankie and I enjoy because we can soak ourselves.

'OK.' Am I OK? My voice comes from somewhere far away, deep in the butcher stall, behind the swinging pig. Quavering, unfamiliar.

I want to tell my mother, to have her comfort me. But there's a strained wariness in her voice that fends me off. She was cross with us for running off, scaring Ah Bing. But it tires her to punish us. That worse may have happened is not something she wants to consider. We should behave better.

On top of the art books, I run my hand along a pencil sketch of my mother's. It's a Chinese village set along a curved bay. On Lamma Island perhaps or Po Toi, sketched lightly as the junk chugs by. There's a traditional row of whitewashed houses. Tiled roofs fishtail prettily in the sun. Quick lines depict the good-luck feng shui woods behind: bamboo, fan palms, lychee trees, an ancient banyan – valuable, lucky trees brought from

China. This village is cheerful, clean, safe.

I think my mother doesn't want to know about me if I'm bad. It's why she doesn't look. Instead, she enlists me, Kate, *muimui*. She needs my help. It's my duty to help keep her world free from Red Guards in back alleys, from Viet Cong passing in the shadows, greasy buckets, snarling dogs. Also, if possible, from Frankie, Frankie's increasing defiance, her disarray.

Frankie's still asleep. But if I go out now, alone, fill the water vases, I'll help maintain the balance of my mother's world.

~   ~   ~

I fill the vase with water from the garden hose. It's a water day and my mother doesn't ask me about the explosion at Lantau. She only asks me to fill the vase. Or maybe, it's my fault. Maybe I turned away too quickly before she could speak. Because I'm scared she won't be able to bear it. We need water for red cat's tails, sweet jasmine, fleshy pink begonias. To keep the flowers alive through the week while people in squatter camps line up at public taps.

'*Maybe next time I'll bring nice lychees for you,*' the pudgy man said.

Along the rim of the vase, the parched clay drinks in water, turning rich and dark. The spray from the hose tears at messy strands of web. A small black spider scurries to the vase's dark mouth for safety. I watch cruelly as it's swept down inside by the torrent. Up on the top floor, the *taitais*, our landlord's mothers, boss each other heedlessly as they scrape a tin water tub across the tile veranda; their high voices wet and slurred because they haven't put in their teeth yet – teeth they keep in mugs of water beside their beds.

The woman killed at Lantau was like the *taitais*. Her teeth flew out as the oilcan exploded. They landed on the path as her body crashed backward into piles of eggplants, ginger, mango, long beans. A boy screamed. The stall blew inward. There was a pool of blood. Dentists can identify dead bodies by their teeth. Sometimes the US Army sends soldiers' teeth back to America for identification. Teeth, a dog-tag, bones, a watch, a pair of glasses, a photograph found in a dead man's pocket in Vietnam. But they don't know who killed him.

The boy's face is covered with scars, raw and ridged, red like the sides of the reservoir. His face is ruined, like the deaf boy's ears. I shut my eyes, imagine I'm walking over to his hospital bed. I see the deaf boy lying there. I run my white fingertips along his scars, wish I could heal them with the magic power of Kuan Yin. 'No! No!' the deaf boy cries. My fingers sting because his skin is so tender.

I'm grateful for the vase with its brown, cracked glaze, large and rounded like a woman's body. Grateful because it smells like earth and it takes a long time to fill. I'm crying and I don't want my mother to see me, or Frankie, and I don't want Ah Bing to see, so I stand with my back to the house, crying and filling the water jug. Filling my mother's body.

At the bottom of the patio wall, big black ants carry the shiny green carcass of a beetle, bite it into pieces to fit through a small crack. Thirsty dragon- and damsel-flies dart back and forth drinking water from the spray. If I stand very still, one will land on my arm, kiss me with blue iridescent wings, bulgy black eyes, lick the sweat from my skin; I can hardly feel it. Would a dragonfly hurt if my skin were burned?

~   ~   ~

When Frankie wakes up she wants a bath. She already used the final bucket of water last night. Now there is more, she wants to bathe again. '*Pak tuali*,' ridiculous, Ah Bing objects. My mother asks her to wait for the evening. That's when we usually take turns sharing our bathwater. But Frankie insists.

I know why. It's because she wants to wash it off, the hands of those men, the smell of raw meat, the blown-up stall. Although she doesn't tell our mother this; she doesn't tell her anything. When it's evening, I refuse to bathe in the same water. I won't touch it.

sixteen

Frankie washes off the fingers of the pudgy man, soaps her mangosteen bosoms, shampoos the smell of meat that clings to her hair.

'He put his hands up my shirt, squeezed my tits,' Frankie says.

The pockmarked man laughed. He held her wrists in one big hand, smothering her mouth with the other. He chuckled while the pudgy man pulled at her waist, writhed against her, grinding his black trousers hard against her thigh.

'The fat man tried to put his hands down my shorts. He tried to touch my vulva, my pubic hair. But my belt was too tight. His fat hand got stuck.' Frankie pauses. Snorts.

'When he fumbled with my buckle, I stamped hard on his foot. At the same time I bit the pockmarked man. I bit so hard, my teeth went right through his skin. I tasted his blood.' She pauses again, not as if she's remembering the taste of blood but as if she's imagining it. Then looks at me as if daring me to challenge her.

'The pimply man swore. He threw me against the dead pig. Next moment, he was kneeling beside me, holding the butcher's knife to my throat.'

I sit on an upturned bucket as she washes. If I lean back against the green-tiled wall, Frankie's body disappears. Then I only see her head, her wet hair dripping over her shoulders, her wild eyes.

Frankie soaps her wrists, her mouth, the insides of her thighs. Yesterday she threw up in the gutter. Yet now she's almost gloating.

'They could have killed me, Kate. Done anything. Instead there was a loud explosion. The fat man shouted and they both ran out.'

It pleases Frankie to say she bit the pockmarked man, drew blood. It shows she's brave, a fighter. The sordidness too pleases her, the smell of meat. Proof that my mother's world is somehow blinkered. The thumbprint bruise on her inner wrist, perfectly formed like an inkstain. Why doesn't my mother see that?

At night, Frankie pulls down her pyjamas to show me where her outer thigh is turning purple-brown. It's where the pudgy man writhed against her, she says. A war wound. War excites her. She likes pulling down her pyjamas, being seen.

seventeen

I need to tell you about my mother's paintings. She paints watercolours of Hong Kong. Landscapes mostly: islands, hillsides, villages, flowers.

She paints the view from the veranda of our house, the sweeping feathery boughs of flame of the forest trees, the sea beyond with junks like wind-borne butterflies. Further out, the receding headlands of Lamma Island, each a paler shade of grey-blue, disappearing into the misty mirage of ancient ink and brush scrolls.

Flame of the forest from Madagascar, bauhinias from India, frangipani from Hawaii, jacarandas and eucalyptus from Australia: my mother paints the shady, flowering, sweet-smelling trees the early settlers brought with them to beautify the barren, dragon-backed hills of Hong Kong. 'Aren't the flame trees gorgeous?' my father says. From our apartment, we look through them to the sea.

My mother paints the terraced rice paddies and vegetable fields in the New Territories, the fish and duck farms near the border at Lok Ma Chau. Sometimes we drive there, up to the hilltop British post, to peer across into China. We train our binoculars, hoping for a glimpse of the Man Po, Chinese Militia, or soldiers of the People's Liberation Army. We fend off hawkers selling fans, hats, slides, grasshoppers made of straw, Mao's Red Books.

At the beginning of July, the Man Po crossed the border at Sha Tau Kok and killed five New Territories policemen. There were rumours of invasion, panicked reports that thousands of PLA troops were massing at the border. Even the cynical McKenna suggested we might leave. Mao could take the colony with a phone call, my father's friends say. China could flood the city with refugees or strangle it by slowly cutting off its piped water supply.

My mother ignores these threats. She's not interested in the smart Gurkha soldiers who man the border, the shadowy figures of PLA far in the distance. Instead she paints the watery chequerboard of fields, ducks bobbing like toy boats. She paints the volcanic peaks of Sai Kung Peninsula, curving like the conical hats of Hoklo fishermen. The steep sway-backed summit of Ma On Shan, Horse Saddle Mountain, Hong Kong's highest peak. She paints the city's colonial buildings: St John's, the Helena May, the Foreign Correspondents' Club, the octagonal cow barns at Dairy Farm. She paints the aqua blue of Miss Tipley's swimming pool, the fragile sprays of St John's lily cascading down the rocky cliff behind.

My mother's paintings are light, pretty, airy. Quickly done. She doesn't make a show of painting. You wouldn't notice that she does it. Charming, Miss Tipley says, picturesque. She shies away from bright colours. Hardly uses them. She rarely paints people, although I keep a pencil sketch she drew of Ah Bing squatting. Concentric circles of rounded shoulders, rounded thighs, wide face, a round bun on the top of a round head. Ah Bing's body, egg-shaped, solid, primal.

And I remember a fanciful painting of the long veranda at

the Repulse Bay Hotel, with curved palms, dots of pink bougainvillea. The small figure at the end is my father. He's sitting back in a rattan chair reading the newspaper, a tiny drink set on the balustrade next to his crossed feet. With only a few brush-strokes, she manages to make him look jaunty, debonair, a man of action at ease, a successful China trader maybe, the proprietor of a rubber plantation. Someone he would like to have been, in another life. A husband she would like to have maybe, one she could bring drinks to and make comfortable.

As soon as she could, my mother escaped her father's tightly run, claustrophobic ministry to go to art school in New York. She met my father at a boat party on Long Island Sound. He was already working for a New York tabloid, regularly getting his photographs on the front page. He was lively and glamorous. They married a year later at my father's farm in Vermont. My mother was twenty. Quietly, she added an extra wedding vow: promising herself that her own marriage would be happier and more serene than her parents' rigid and fretful wedlock.

My mother's paintings are nostalgic, suggestive. They conjure a mythical past, an alternative present, one my father would be happy to indulge in if it wasn't for the war. A world she'd like us, her children, to believe in too.

Her China is a land of Karst Mountains where Taoist hermits bent over gnarly canes climb for ever to high temples swathed in mists, where soft-spoken scholars drink tea in pavilions, recite their verses in melodious Mandarin instead of the crude, guttural Cantonese of Hong Kong. It's ethereal, ancient, the land of the Forbidden City. Not this other China gone mad, slamming its doors to the West, cutting off pigtails, sending bodies downriver.

Her Hong Kong resembles nineteenth-century China trade paintings where pith-helmeted sahibs ride on rattan chairs and silent natives pass in quaint straw hats. They are not unlike the playful sketches of George Chinnery, an Irishman, who depicted the faded charm of nearby Macau. There are no fleshy periwinkles in her paintings, no seaborne garbage. There are no cuts and scratches that sting in the saltwater. No smell of dried fish. No body floating up in the sea.

There's nothing to show she understands us, Frankie and me, that she loves us anyway. There are no imperfections.

~   ~   ~

It's my mother's ability to transform her surroundings that explains why we stay in Hong Kong. Why we don't desert the colony for 'home leave' or 'summer hols' like most other expatriates, jetting off from Kai Tak on Cathay Pacific, BOAC, TWA – even the Chief of Police. And the beleaguered Governor, waylaid in Japan with the flu, leaving his number two, the Deputy Colonial Secretary, in charge.

'Marianne, you simply can't stay in Hong Kong with all the trouble, dear. Everyone's leaving. Besides, it's simply too hot,' British wives advise my mother at cocktail parties, coddling her with the arrogance of a nation more experienced in colonial life. They underestimate my mother's will, her ability to simply shut out the Red Guards, bombs, water shortages, invasion. Stuff them under books. Pretend they don't exist. It's why we aren't sitting around my father's farm in Vermont barbecuing hamburgers, drinking iced tea.

There's another reason, of course. She's afraid my father might leave. He might become so intoxicated with the war that he forgets us. There are plenty of diplomats, photographers, hacks, McKenna for instance, who've left their wives, fallen in love with Vietnamese women, or just with the war itself. Or with the country, green as a parrot's wing. Husbands, fathers who don't come home any more. Or come home in body bags.

If you consider them, the possibilities are frightening. Better turn the other way, see the world through feathery boughs, dots of pink bougainvillea, headlands that recede one into another, junk sails like tattered butterflies. It's a means of survival. If you can manage it.

eighteen

The smell of drying fish is strong and sharp. It reaches you as you come up from the beach, before you walk into the village. Rows and rows of small fish, laid out on rattan mats in the hot sun.

An old woman peers at us from inside a darkened doorway, sitting behind a raised portal built to keep out bad spirits. Half-naked children run before us like heralds, shouting, '*Gwailo. Gwailo.*' White ghosts. White ghosts. Scrawny chickens peck underfoot, unbothered. A mangy chow rushes at us from the shade of a banyan, teeth bared. Whiny Cantonese love songs trickle from a transistor radio. '*Gwailo. Gwailo,*' the children cry. The dog snarls.

The village consists of two rows of whitewashed houses made of mud brick. Inside, the houses are cool and dark with no windows. They have curving green-tiled roofs. Beyond the hot courtyards spread with fish are fields of vegetables, neatly tended, reeking of human night soil. There is a central man-made pond, an ancient pump for watering. Plastic bags tied on sticks keep the birds off.

Frankie and I walk through, stepping warily as we pass the dog. Just off the path beyond the village, we dip through the broken door of a ruined church, its glass windows shattered, walls streaked green with mould. An iron cross rusts over a crumbling door. Inside it's quiet. The roof's fallen in, the aisles are filled with rubble. Jasmine and honeysuckle clamber over the once ornate blue-and-white plaster altar, smelling wanton, seductive.

The children don't follow us here. They skip off, back to the village. Perhaps they're afraid of our *gwailo* God, of the stories their parents tell of a tall, gaunt priest striding forth in funereal white robes, cursing their earth gods and kitchen gods, scowling at their joss sticks. Father Simeon Volunteri, my father tells us, was a nineteenth-century Italian missionary from Milan. He built the church, his heart set on taming the Sai Kung pirates.

Abandoned places are our territory, ours for entering, taking. We're archaeologists, hermit crabs, Viet Cong scouts, Volunteri's followers. Saying nothing, we shuffle along the aisle, searching for some relic, some Italian talisman. An olive-wood cross. A piece of wild boarskin. The church exudes a silence, a reverence for Volunteri, his passion, as if breathing a final sigh before submitting to the more ancient rhythms of the village, the tangled vines of jungle.

How he raged when he saw the pirates, returning home with crates of opium, silver, tea, taken from European ships. When he refused to cook rice, free meals, a tactic his mission in China had used, his converts stopped coming. He stormed around their small Tin Hau Temple. I imagine he went mad. Disappeared into the jungle. How could he survive, a lone white man with his mission, his desire? Even if he learned Chinese, he would never know all its secrets.

Frankie motions for me to crouch quickly under the arched window. We've run ahead. We'll hide here while the others go by, wait for my father, who's home. 'On R&R,' he calls it.

Peering out through a splintered shutter that hangs on a rusty hinge, through bits of gold and blue glass, we hear Trung, the Chinese wife of his colleague Lewis, explaining how the villagers ferment the dried fish, send it to a small bottling factory in Sai Kung village. Beside her, our mother, High Auntie – a tall New Yorker nicknamed by Ah Bing – and Humphries, an English friend, listen eagerly, anxious to learn the secrets of the Sai Kung pirates subdued through the city's appetite for fishpaste.

Frankie pushes my shoulder down. Our father, striding in front of the others, bears down on us. He's exposed himself to enemy fire, I think, although he almost got by without us noticing. Hiding behind the broken shutter, I see without a doubt that he's the key target. You can tell from his step, he's commander of the troops, father of the flock. But before either of us can take aim, he stops at our window. He's seen us. Our father, thin, gaunt, distracted, his eyes blazing, wild like Volunteri, about to expose us. What will he say?

I'll surrender, emerge arms-up out of my foxhole, confess my sins, proclaim my everlasting devotion even without the rice bowls. I love you, Dad. Love me. Forgive me. But Frankie's hand holds me back. It seems he hasn't found us after all. He's merely stopped here to tear a branch from a bush. Secretly, we watch him struggle because the branch won't give. It only tears along wet strands of fibre without breaking.

As the others approach, my father's determination grows awkward, almost desperate as he tugs and wrenches at the stubborn leaves. Finally, he remembers the jackknife he keeps in his pocket, tied to his belt loop with a shoelace. He extracts the blade and cuts the fleshy branch. The others bottle up behind him on the path but he doesn't make way. Puzzled, they wait as he hacks the branch into pieces, sticks the foliage into his straw hat and smiles.

'Michael!' High Auntie titters. He strides past us, smiling. Safe now. Camouflaged. He's Viet Cong.

'If we were American soldiers, we could have killed him,' I say.

nineteen

Why do I think of killing my father? Because he walks past us in the abandoned church and doesn't see us. He doesn't see how Frankie sits too close to Humphries in the darkening light. Doesn't notice how she laughs too loud, edges over too close. How Humphries' hand brushes the tops of her thighs as he reaches for more barbecued ribs. I watch closely. But no one's watching me.

It's getting dark, the last glow of sun that makes people's faces look as if they were in firelight. Lewis, Trung, High Auntie, a contingent of the crowd that appears when my father's home. Friends suddenly willing to take off days on end though they don't see us the rest of the time, or maybe my mother doesn't ask them. Always a group because my father needs an audience, bodyguards, to protect him from us, his family. It's only when he's away that we're alone.

Frankie and Humphries sit up on the rail of the junk, a little outside the magic circle. The plates on their laps hide the way Humphries' knuckles press into the flesh of her thigh. Humphries is a grown-up, twice Frankie's age. He has tight, curly hair, a neat moustache that gives him a rakish look. An infectious laugh. Behind them, hills, some startlingly sharp, volcanic, darken into abstract shapes. Stars emerge in the still-light sky.

My father's voice is low, excitable, fresh from the war. 'Elizabeth's radio station wanted background noises. We sat round at the Caravelle. Salzman did incoming. McKenna, machine gun. Simon, cicadas at night. We joined forces for the jungle: insects, frogs, bursts of gunfire. I did gibbons. There are hordes of gibbons in the Central Highlands. Salzman the whack of a Huey's propeller blades.' When he speaks, we lean closer, stop talking. He's the one who's seen it, up close, taken photographs. The war we read about in the newspaper. And we want to see it too, smell it, hear it, feel it. The bodies, the guns, the sickly red globs of burning napalm, the whack of a Huey's blades, earth-shattering explosions of seven-hundred-and-fifty-pound bombs. And Saigon too, the Caravelle, the Continental, Cercle Sportif, the farcical press briefings at Army head-quarters – 'five o'clock follies' – where US colonels spin webs of numbers and acronyms. The notorious bars on Tu Do Street, pretty girls, Frankie's and my age, the city's throb of rot, corruption, poverty and enchantment. We want that too. Because it's where life is right now, and death. Not up on the railing where Frankie crassly opens her legs so her skin touches Humphries.

Only my mother looks away from him, aloof, a little sad. The more stories he tells, the harder it is to reach him.

'There was a boy I photographed at the Red Cross Amputee Centre in Saigon,' my father says. 'He was lying on a board cot in a sweltering tin shed reading, of all things, *Catcher in the Rye*.

'I wanted to ask him how he'd been hurt and how long he'd been waiting for an artificial leg. They have to wait months and months. But before I could speak, he starts asking me about the relationship between Holden Caulfield and Phoebe. Had I read *The Great Gatsby*? How did I think Hemingway would have treated the fighting at Ia Drang? We must have talked for an hour. But when I developed the picture, I realized I hadn't even written down the boy's name, nor his age. McKenna was furious because *Time* wanted to use the photo, as a half-page spread.'

Frankie wants to attract Humphries, make him put his hands on her skin, up the leg of her shorts, show her she's noticed, desirable. She wants him to unbutton her shorts, touch her where the pudgy man failed to.

'How are the Americans going to handle Ky in the September elections?' Humphries asks, leaning forward and removing his knuckles from Frankie's thigh as if they had merely rested there by mistake. 'He's been a disaster as Prime Minister. When Buddhist monks pour out into the streets to demonstrate, it's a real embarrassment for the US, isn't it? Makes it look as if South Vietnam itself is in a state of civil war.'

At the bow, I hear Ah Bing cackle loudly. One of the crew chides her for her bossiness. Self-appointed expert on the ways of *gwailos*, she lords it over the foredeck. Delivers a stream of directions as the three men squat around the small stove, cooking ribs and fish and oily *bok choi*. More ginger, too much oil, she scolds them, even though she herself is a terrible cook. They're too wasteful, they'll burn the fish. The *gwailos* won't like it if it's overdone.

Ah Bing never eats with us when our parents are home. Her manners are coarse. She shovels food into her mouth instead of picking it up with chopsticks. She talks through mouthfuls of food. We'll eat like her given half a chance. We'll sidle up to older men so our bare thighs touch their thick legs. Because our father doesn't see us. We're invisible. Heathens. *Gwaimuis*, little white ghosts. *Houh hoi*, whores. Humphries' legs look pale and hairy next to Frankie's. He wears blue cotton shorts. My father's legs are sinewy, slightly bowed, burned red-brown. His shorts are khaki, British military.

'Come closer, Katenick,' my father urges me gently. Perhaps he knows I want to kill him. I'm a threat, a Viet Cong plant, an unpredictable pawn like Prime Minister Ky. Only he'll offer a truce, subdue me.

'You won't mind if I eat this piece of gristle, will you?' He picks the last rib from my plate. It's his excuse but I know better. What he really wants is my attention; he's asking for my unquestioned devotion, my faith. He's Volunteri. And even as I move along the bench, I forgive him, offer up my food. Because now I'm closest of all. I smell the war. The way he takes the rib from my plate without even waiting for an answer shows how close we are. I know he likes the gristly bits best. I know how he wants to be loved. I'm his daughter. It's Frankie's fault if she wants to rub her thighs against Humphries on the railing, not his. Not my mother's.

As I edge closer to him, Frankie clambers noisily over the railing, her feet touching the water, splashing it. 'There's no moon tonight. Let's see if there's phosphorescence.' Dramatically she lets her legs slip and she falls, clasping first at the rail, then at Humphries, which is her purpose really. She's punishing him for removing his hand. Or she's trying to distract our father from me. Look at me, Dad. I'm the one clawing Humphries. I'm the one who needs you.

Humphries smiles down at her, a big girl, not quite a girl but not a woman either, hanging from his belt. Trying to pull him in on top of her. Everyone laughs, except my mother who leans forward, straightening the serving plates.

Then Humphries curtly removes Frankie's hands and drops

her into the water. What does she expect? What could he possibly do with her in front of everyone? The girl's trouble.

'Pig!' Frankie splutters as she comes up for air. Her legs thrash trails of light in the water. My father chews the gristly fat of my rib.

~   ~   ~

Later in the night, Frankie throws her heavy leg over my thighs and whispers hot in my ear. We're lying on mattresses spread out over the floor of the cabin. Rattan sides are rolled up on either side to let in the sea breeze.

'He put his hand right up near my crotch,' Frankie breathes incredulously. 'It's so gross. Don't you think so?'

I hide in the dark. Don't say anything, hope she won't make me. How can she act so prudish when I saw her rub her leg against him, clutch at him as she fell over the side? Doesn't she know what will happen? Didn't she tell me how the pudgy man tried to touch her? How the other man held a knife to her throat?

'He probably would have touched it if I hadn't jumped overboard.' Jumped! Is that how she expects me to see it? Frankie, the chaste maiden, throwing herself overboard to escape the arms of a lecherous villain? Not to see how Humphries dropped her in the water, her legs and arms flailing indecorously?

I roll over, angry with my older sister for not admitting what we know. For making me see too much, then asking me to pretend it didn't happen. I open my eyes. Suddenly I remember what I wanted to tell my father. Why I wanted to kill him. It's my story trapped inside me. The body rising from the sea. The man with his pink tongue, his fleshy hands. The bag of lychees, too heavy. I'm scared of the pudgy man, scared of the woman who died, the burned boy. And now I want to kill my father because he surrounds himself with so many people and adventures and stories that I will never reach him, never be able to tell him what happened to Frankie and me. And life is the war. It's not Lantau, not the butcher stall. Because much worse things happen there – in Vietnam.

Past the rattan shades are shapes of dark hills, sharp points of stars. Cigar smoke trickles down from the deck, where my father, Humphries and Lewis sit smoking. The tips of their cigars light the dark.

Later, when the women come to sleep, Trung lets down her hair like night falling into the boat. In a corner, my mother struggles to remove her bra and pants under her nightgown, so we don't see her naked in the dark.

My father, Lewis, Humphries, the crew sleep up on deck. Low voices, hushed. If I listen, I hear the names of far-off places – Ia Drang, Pleiku, Khe Sanh – wash back and forth in the creaking of the boat, the lull of the waves. 'The worst the grunts say is when you get incoming just when you open your C-ration. You don't want to get hit but you don't want to fall all over your stew either.'

If I listen, I hear my father, suddenly awake, plunging off the stern, whooping in the dark of the night before he hits the sea. I breathe in the sharp smell of mould from the mattresses.

Maybe my father will stay up when the others go to bed, wait for me, Katenick. Maybe if I wake up early, he'll be there, alone. Then I'll put down my gun and tell him. I'll ask him to sit cross-legged with me on the temple patio, listen to the BBC. Tell him to wrap us in woollen sweaters despite the desperate heat, decipher our fortunes. Then he'll tell me it's OK. It isn't our fault. We are too small and not looked after. Then he'll kiss Frankie and put his arm around her so she won't have to rub legs with Humphries in the dark. We'll watch bodies like glow-worms rise up from the sea.

twenty

When Frankie tells me what happened to her in the butcher shop, she doesn't ask about the lychees. She never mentions them again. Maybe she believes it was just a bag of fruit. She's not the one who searches out and reads the newspaper. Maybe she thinks I don't know and she doesn't want to be the one to tell me.

More likely it frightens her, what I did. It threatens Frankie's position too. Because Frankie sets herself up as warrior, fighter, heroine, victim, all combined. I'm just supposed to be Katenick, *muimui*, little sister, follower, sidekick.

What happens to Frankie is the important story, the one that consumes her and our family that summer. Even though no one speaks of it. Even later, we never say it out loud. The lychees, the bomb at the market become my secret. One I cannot tell.

twenty-one

The picture of my father with his camouflaged Viet Cong hat reminds me of another image I had forgotten. Many years later, when I am grown up with children of my own, I am living in the same city as Lewis and Trung. One day Lewis calls up to invite me to dinner. He's come across some old home movie he filmed using my father's Super-8 camera. He thought I might like to see them.

At first, I'm surprised when I see Lewis. He's shorter than I thought, wiry, intense. He's aged, too, ravaged. Trung is elegant, slender, composed, the way I remember her. She holds out her arms.

'Katie-ah. How nice to see you. Such a long time.'

After dinner, Trung brings hot jasmine tea and settles herself on the sofa next to me. Lewis doesn't rush her. He fine-tunes the projector, focuses. A square of bright light illuminates the slide screen. Then a picture, a beach with mountains.

'Tai Long Wan,' Big Wave Bay, Lewis says, as if I've forgotten.

I don't tell him I keep maps and charts on my walls like my father. That even if I shut my eyes, I can see the long, pristine stretch of sand. Beaches spread beneath precipitous green hills, nestling between the rocky arms of jagged rhyolite peninsulas. Sai Wan, Ham Tin Wan, Tai Wan, Tung Wan, I know their names.

I can run my fingers along this coast. Up lines marking streams that run down from the hillsides, washing into fetid tide pools. A bridge with rickety planks, a loose rope to hold on to, lead back into paddy fields stinking of human night soil, Volunteri's church, to villages and mangrove swamps tangled as dreams. Perhaps there's a cave, the water rushes in and out echoing.

'You remember Sai Kung Peninsula, up in the Northeast New Territories?' Lewis asks. 'Your father liked to rent an old sailing junk and take us all along.'

The *Sea Dragon*. The jerky camera traces her ungainly lines from the low bow up to her high stern. Along the large wooden boom, towels and clothes hang to dry over loosely furled brown sails.

There on the cushioned bench along the stern, my mother sits demurely, her legs folded to one side. Even in the heat, she's careful about how she looks. Next to her, High Auntie sits reading a book by Allen Ginsberg.

The screen blinks and shows again a white stretch of beach. Flat, naked sand smoothed by the sea, unblemished except where tunnelling sand mites toss up wet pellets. It's long enough to run until you can't breathe and still you haven't covered half of it. In the distance, I stoop to pick up a cowrie shell, or the chalk-soft bone of a cuttlefish, sun-bleached, tapered like a seed.

Me. Trung. High Auntie. Ah Bing squats fully clothed in the sea, her white shirt blotted wet. The camera zooms in on Ah Bing's full, wide face. Her gold teeth flash in the sun. Ah Bing believes photographs are taken for ancestor worship so she's pleased to be filmed, but also a little wary of the frivolous nature of *gwailo* picture-taking.

Suddenly the image is obstructed, broken apart by blurry

hands and feet, too close for the lens's focus. It's Frankie. She turns a cartwheel right up to the camera, face, arms, legs twirling on the screen as if she would come right out. Gently, Trung lays her hand on my shoulder, comforting, making sure it's all right for me to see Frankie. Lewis looks away. At night, we eat with bare hands under an open sky.

Lewis's movie is black and white, marred by spots of mildew from being stored too long in the Far East. It jumps and shudders as it feeds through the projector. The motor clickety-clacks. I tuck my feet under me.

On the screen Trung is swimming, a graceful breast-stroke, her black hair piled like a pagoda on top of her head. She carries it carefully as if she's rescuing it from her country. A pagoda she can unpin, letting her hair tumble down.

Another blink. Then the camera pans across the beach, aimlessly, as if Lewis has left it on by mistake. No, it's a large hole he's filming, surrounded by a mound of upturned sand. The camera lingers, waiting to catch something, an animal perhaps, a fugitive.

A thin figure rises, wild, unshaven, holding something in his hand. A ball of sand. It's my father. He holds the ball away from his body as if it's alive or dangerous, pulls an imaginary ring, and throws. His back is dark and bare. His arm swings out. It's a grenade. It's going to explode. It's going to hit us. My father dives for cover and disappears.

I'm startled by how young, how thin my father is, fragile. He looks like I do now. But harder, more weathered and faraway. His hair is ruffled and unkempt. Dark stubble on his cheeks. It's like the time he cut the branches to camouflage his hat. He's Viet Cong again, impersonating the enemy. He's not at Sai Kung at all but somewhere along the Indochina coast, staying low to avoid incoming. Perhaps he's dug a whole tunnel system under the beach. We'll never find him.

~　　~　　~

Maybe it's unfair the way I remember it. Maybe I'm too hard on my father. Maybe my memory exaggerates. Maybe he knew everything. He just couldn't help us. Like we couldn't help him. He hides in tunnels, behind his camera lenses, like I hide in the dark from Frankie, don't answer her questions, pretend to be asleep.

~　　~　　~

'Lew cracked. The Embassy sent him home,' my father says on his next leave. He says this to my mother in an offhand way as if Lewis has been dismissed from school. Given detention. Cracked isn't what a grown-up does. Or even what a child is supposed to do. I'm eavesdropping so I can't ask what he means. I think Frankie is cracking. I can't ask about that either.

Maybe my father's not really offhand. Maybe he's just protecting himself. Pretending it doesn't matter. Maybe he's cracking too. He's got a photograph on the front cover of *Time* magazine of a Marine crouching, covering his head, mud flung up like paint as the earth explodes around him.

"'If your pictures aren't good enough, you're not close enough,'" he quotes the war photographer Robert Capa. Capa was blown up in Vietnam, when he stepped out of a French truck on to a land mine.

Lewis worked for the Embassy in Saigon. It was his job to keep track of military actions, the numbers of dead, the body counts, the kill ratios. To obfuscate his reports with official acronyms or military jargon: KIAs, KBAs, MIA, NVC, DMZ, R&R, 'Enemy engagement' when a Viet Cong sniper kills ten Americans before being shot out of his tree, 'Enemy infrastructure' to describe a village of straw huts. When he speaks to relatives from the US, he's supposed to use a kindly, bereaved voice he can hardly stand.

My father's job is to take photographs. To show things the way they are. He doesn't have to say a word if he doesn't want to.

twenty-two

Did I tell you my father loves Saigon? He finds it enchanting: the cyclos, the sampans, the breeze coming down the river at night. He loves the smells. He loves the sweat on his own body. He's never sweated so much before.

In Saigon, my father wears white shirts. He drinks Pernod or cassis on the open terrace at the Continental Palace Hotel with other journalists, or on the roof of the Majestic, or at the Cercle Sportif. He eats Palourdes Bolognese at a restaurant with murals of Basque fishermen painted with Vietnamese faces. Sometimes he goes to Cholon, to the Arc en Ciel or other clubs. He takes his camera with him.

This is the East he read about in Greene, and Maugham and Conrad. When a car backfires, the journalists rush out to the street just as they did in Greene's day, he says. It might be a bomb. They carry copies of *The Quiet American* in their back pockets. He takes Saigon Duck for a bath.

In Saigon, my father has to push his way through gangs of children who wait at the entrance of his hotel. 'Give money. Give money,' the children beg. They are refugees whose older sisters work the bars along Tu Do Street. GI bars with neon names like Wild West, Rainbow, Melody, Papillon. Girls no older than me and Frankie, whose fathers look the other way because their daughters make more in a night than they can make in months. Outside the cathedral, crippled beggars hobble forward, their legs blown off by land mines. Young mothers hold up their hands for money.

Once when two children ran at my father, he believed for a moment that they were the ghosts of children he had just photographed blown up along a paddy dyke. 'Viet Cong,' the sergeant grunted in self-defence as he kicked at the basket the children had been carrying. The basket was full of shrapnel, bits of metal the Viet Cong use for packing bombs. The children's chests were blown open. Their faces splattered with bits of heart and lung. A young soldier threw up in the paddy field. My father took photographs.

At times, he thinks of his own father, how he came back from World War II, drunken, abusive, remote. Never talking of the things he'd seen.

Let me tell you this. In Saigon, my father smells dead bodies in his room at the Continental. The first time it happens, he tries to wash off the smell, tries to wash the insides of his nostrils with Dial soap. He lights a cigarette and blows the smoke through his nose. After that, he just feels it coming. He's resigned to it. He lies in bed under the mosquito net and waits for the smell. The only thing he can do is go back out to the field. Fresh bodies to make the old ones stop smelling.

~   ~   ~

Did I tell you my father wears Marine fatigues in the field? All the journalists and photographers do. He wears Marine-issued fatigues, boots, a helmet. He carries a canteen covered with olive-green canvas. He accompanies Marine patrols, sleeps in

Marine bunkers, catches rides in Marine helicopters, eats C-rations, boils his coffee with a pinch of C4 explosive. The only things that are his own are his cameras, his notebooks, the cigarettes he keeps tucked under the strap of his helmet and a tiny bronze Buddha in his pocket. Because of his cameras, he's afraid the Viet Cong will mistake him for the radio man and take him out first.

In the field, he doesn't carry a gun, though sometimes he'd like to. Not because he believes in the war but because he wants to get close. Sometimes keeping alive is the only thing that makes sense. Then he envies the grunts with their guns. Then he wants a gun, not a camera. So, I'm not the only one who wants a gun.

twenty-three

Towards the end of that summer, my parents decided to send Frankie away to boarding school. We weren't sure why. I don't remember our parents announcing their decision. I don't remember any discussion, any questions, reassurances. It is just something we know one day, something that happens to girls Frankie's age when their parents live overseas. What she needs is a better school, more structure, more sport, my mother says.

But I think the real reason is that my mother's scared of her, and tired too. Scared of the way Frankie is: physical, close, overheated, tormenting. The way she demands a testament of unconditional love – I love you no matter what – which she never gets. The way she refuses to go along.

'They're sending me away,' Frankie complains. 'I don't want to go.' We're at our secret hideout behind the apartment, the ruined foundation overtaken by jungle. Frankie has carried up a ripe yellow pomelo, split open, from the garden. We shred its sections, popping the individual pulps between our teeth like monkeys.

'Maybe you could tell them you want to stay. They can't force you,' I begin weakly.

'She doesn't want me,' Frankie says.

We both heard our mother's words. We crouched in the hall

outside her closed door, listening to what she told our father. 'She's too wild, too unruly. She goes about half-naked. Spends all her time alone with Kate or Ah Bing, speaking pidgin. The school here's second-rate. She'll fall behind.'

'Maybe she thinks you'll like it better there,' I say. I know it's disingenuous. Frankie wants to stay here, in the jungle with me, lying on silk scarves, smoking cigarettes, sucking the tangy pulp of pomelo. At the end of the summer, she wants to return with me to our second-rate school, with its long verandas, mouldy classrooms, rain cascading down drains. She wants to play netball in the small cement playground where palms and elephant leaves press in against the wire fence. Spend our fifty-cent pieces on ice lollies and blackcurrant pastilles at the tuck shop. Play 'tig' with our British classmates. Girls in Frankie's class who shorten their skirts, hang their arms around boys, smoke cigarettes under a bridge along Bowen Path.

The Prisoner of War School, we call it. The building was a hospital where the Japanese interned sickly POWs. Ah Bing says the Japanese tortured and killed patients there, ones who wouldn't tell them things. People heard screaming. Just beyond the playground, she points out where the hospital incinerator and morgue once stood.

Sometimes at lunch, I go to the library. The deaf boy is there. He sits at a long wooden table, reading a book, *The Ecology of the Hong Kong Seashore*. Along the shelves are three crumbling volumes of Scottish history, a *Young Ladies' Guide to Dressage and Riding Etiquette*. When the deaf boy looks up at me, the pages of his book flip backwards and forwards in the wake of a large, standing fan. He doesn't notice because he can't hear.

'She's scared of me,' Frankie says. 'I'm not like you. I don't do what she says. She's scared I might even get you in trouble.'

You already have, I think. It's because of you I'm secret sister, guardian, bearer of secrets heavy as lychees. When we go out with Ah Bing, I keep a lookout for the men from Lantau. I feel nauseous when I see a policeman.

I wish I could walk over to the deaf boy, gently close his book. I'd like to touch his face, the way I would touch the burned boy's if I could. I think these things but don't say them.

Is it because of me they're sending her away, to protect me? Without Frankie, who am I?

'I don't want you to go,' I say.

'They can't force me.'

~   ~   ~

It's because they're sending her away that Frankie becomes more reckless, more desperate. If she gets in enough trouble, they'll have to keep her, let her stay. Maybe they'll realize she's not ready to go off on her own; she needs looking after, their protection. The butcher shop was only the beginning.

My father doesn't see us. He doesn't come with us to the temple to hear Ah Sun chant our fortunes. That's why Frankie flirts with my father's friends, Humphries, Pym, and leans too close, falling against them when she giggles, sneaking sips of wine from their glasses. It's because she has to compete. With Vietnam, pronounced *nahm* (not *nam*) with a soft, redolent *ah*. Vietnahm with its parrot-green fields, jungle-covered hills, its translucent caves where Buddhas swim, its children burned by napalm. Their clothes dissolve under searing jelly, their skin bubbles.

Look at me, notice me, love me, Frankie cries. No one hears. Friends laugh. This is something that happens to girls Frankie's age. No need to worry. It's not her country that's under attack. It's not her village burning. And soon she'll be going to boarding school. In this way, my mother plans to extract her primly from the mess she's getting herself into. The same way Humphries pries her hands off him on the junk and drops her in the sea.

'Pig!' Frankie splutters, her legs thrashing trails of phosphorescence. Why does she have to be so demanding, so selfish, so present?

twenty-four

We're out for dinner at the Royal Hong Kong Yacht Club. Frankie flirts with Pym, a large, loud, British detective who laughs and looks at her with surprise. Frankie insists on wearing blue jeans, a tie-dyed shirt. I'm wearing a stretchy skirt and a blue-and-white striped T-shirt. My mother wears short ivory trousers and a pale green silk shirt with a high collar and Chinese buttons.

Tables with pressed linen cloths are set on the tiled veranda outside. Up on the stone railing, a small replica of Copenhagen's Little Mermaid looks across water dark and slick with diesel oil. The lights from the restaurant illuminate plastic bags and discarded chicken bones floating on the waves. A plane approaches Kai Tak Airport across the harbour.

'Thai Airways. The eight o'clock flight from Bangkok,' my father notes. A dog howls from the mass of junks and sampans that crowd into Causeway Bay Typhoon Shelter beyond the row of gleaming white yachts. Pym stands up to check the plane's tail colours. My father's right, of course. He knows all the flights, in and out.

Pym would take Frankie up on her offer if he wanted. But after dinner, he heads to the main bar, a big echoey room where sailing trophies line the walls. No children allowed, a sign says.

That includes Frankie and me. The women hang back too, lingering over teas and coffees, breathing in the damp, malodorous air of the harbour, talking about amahs and parties, someone who's left his wife. My mother sits back. She's quieter than the others. Prettier too.

Through the door, I can see Pym demonstrating a new seltzer-maker, spraying it lewdly while the Chinese barman stands to one side smiling. My father is telling stories. Tonight, there's a movie: *The Mudlark*, which is why my parents have brought us. The movie's about to begin but now I can't find Frankie. I see that Humphries isn't around either.

I walk alone to the chart room, where the movie's showing, sit by myself in the dark halfway up towards the screen. It's a story of an orphan named Wheeler who lives by scavenging the muddy banks of the Thames. One day, he comes across a dead seaman and finds, in the sailor's pocket, a medallion with an image of Queen Victoria. Taking to heart the words, *Mother of all England*, he sets off across the grey, cold streets of London to find her. When he slips down a coal chute into Windsor Castle, his face becomes black – he's a savage.

It's that other world, the West, the world I come from. I know its stories, its heroes and heroines, and yet I know I'm different too. I'm more like the wild man that frightens them: Queequeg, Man Friday, a cannibal. The girl pirate in *High Wind in Jamaica*. If they took me back now, I'd be Ram Dass, the Indian servant poking his head out of the London skylight for a glimpse of the sky, not the little Princess who sees him. I'd be like Wheeler, a scavenger, only they wouldn't be able to wash the coal dust off my face.

Where is Frankie? I wait for her. What will I say if my mother comes in and she's not here?

~ ~ ~

'Humphries took me down to the bowling room,' Frankie tells me in the dark. We're lying in our beds. The metal-framed windows, open wide, admit the low mating calls of frogs, the high-pitched shrieking of cicadas. The ceiling fan chops the hot air above us. I've been out with a flashlight, to find them congregated around Ah Fu's ornamental pond: big lumpy bullfrogs with swelling throats, three-quarters submerged in the still brown water, striped paddy frogs and smaller peeping tree frogs. Their sticky toes cling to the porcelain figurines Ah Fu has arranged in the crevices of the pond's miniature mountain. In a jagged cave, the Eight Immortal Fairies; on a cliff, the Taoist Lao Tzu riding a water buffalo; on a low outcrop, bearded Confucius.

Frankie lies with her pyjama top open. Her breasts splay provocatively to either side. Not mangosteens, I think, more like papayas, overripe, rotting. I pull the thin sheet over my hot body to hide myself from her.

'He unzipped his trousers and put my hands on his penis. I rubbed them back and forth,' Frankie informs me. 'Ugh. He got all stiff and then his sperm squirted out down his leg.'

He must have had to wash it off, I think. If his trousers were wet, he must have had to pretend he'd spilled a drink. Or, if he was nimble, he could have sprayed himself on purpose with Pym's seltzer-maker. Frankie laughs. I'm quiet. Humphries is younger than my father but much older than us. I know he shouldn't do this.

Are they true, the things she tells me? Or is she just trying to shock me? Did she really bite the pockmarked man?

'Did he do anything else?'

'No!' Frankie spits back, as if I'd insulted her. 'What do you think I am?'

What are you? Who are you? Who am I? It's what I'm trying to figure out. Maybe Frankie is seeking her revenge for what the pudgy man did to her in the butcher shop. Maybe she wants to hurt Humphries, get him in trouble.

'How did Humphries clean it off?'

'I don't care,' says Frankie. 'It's his mess. Girls don't come like that.'

I do care. It's important to me. If I'm Frankie's alibi, her confidante, her bodyguard, it's up to me to make sure she doesn't get caught. To keep watch. It's my job to clean up after her. Why does she have to tell me these things?

twenty-five

Ah Bing hates men. When my father walks into the kitchen, she scoffs, 'Nobody here!' He gets himself a bowl of nuts and goes out quickly. It's impressive how easy it is for her to intimidate him. When she was a girl, only four years old, her father died. Left her mother with five children to feed. If he hadn't died, her mother would never have sent her away. Twice, her mother sent her away to live with another family. Both times, she ran home.

In China, there were ducks on the pond. When she was small, she'd run down and chase them. *Raanc. Raanc.* They flew off to the other side. In China, Auntie had a big pig, black and hairy. Her brothers poked it with a stick. It squealed.

Her brothers, *po!* They were other no-good men. Opium Kuan, Opium Dum, she calls them. Smoking made them weak and thin like old ladies. She should have known how they'd turn out from the way they poked Auntie's pig. Later, they sold the clothes off their children's backs to pay for their pipes. Then when they had taken everything, they left their wives, her sisters-in-law, and disappeared. She heard they went to Hong Kong. They might as well be dead for all she cares.

~   ~   ~

The needle pricks her finger as she pushes it through the shirt she's sewing. The material's from one of my mother's discarded dresses. Piles of our unwanted, outgrown clothes under Ah Bing's bed. She keeps them all because she knows what we don't know. How there are naked children, neglected children. Children who've never had a new pair of pyjamas, who are sent away, mistreated by families who don't love them. Like orphans, they are never given the best food. If the Japanese come, or the Communists, I tell her, we could live for weeks on the things under her bed.

Men, *po*! They're lazy and stupid. Look at your father. He has a good job. He takes photographs for an American magazine. But he can't even cook an egg, iron a shirt. If he wants something he always asks, 'Where's Marianne? Where's Marianne?'

Remember the last time he kept shivering? 'Ah Bing, do you know where my sweater is? It's so cold.' So cold in this heat? He is too thin, thin as if he's been smoking. But he hasn't. White men don't smoke opium. He's cold because of the war. The war in Vietnam.

She left China before the Japanese came. But they caught up with her in Singapore. She had to leave her missee's house. Her friends told her it wasn't safe. They said the Japanese would cut off her head if they found her working for a foreigner. 'Don't go. Don't go,' her missee pleaded. 'Wait till my husband gets back.' Her missee held back her wages to try to make Ah Bing stay. If the Japanese bombed, they could hide under a table. Then Kuan Yin came to her in a dream. Told her to go. When she returned a week later, the house was gone, bombed. She never saw her missee again. She never got her last month's wages.

In Vietnam, it's Ho Chi Minh, the Viet Cong. In China, it's Mao, the Red Guards.

Auntie's pig squealed when they cut its throat but the Red Guards were only young, they didn't know how to slaughter a pig. It broke loose from them and ran around the garden, splattering blood everywhere. Auntie screamed until they hit her. Uncle turned his head. He couldn't do anything. They had tied his hands behind his back.

'Nobody here! Go away.' She is nobody because her mother sent her away. The Red Guards took her temple. Go away. Get your own sweater. Your own bowl of nuts. Bad things happen. Why do you want to go to Vietnam to find them?

~   ~   ~

Ah Bing's got a filthy tongue. My mother doesn't know half the things she says. '*Diu ke lo si*,' go have sex with your old teacher. The common curse is '*lo mo*', with your mother, but Ah Bing switches it around because she doesn't like men. This is just a light-hearted, everyday curse, the way we say, 'Damn' or 'Christ'. When she's really cross, she says, '*Ham ga chang*,' may all your descendants and ancestors be obliterated. She calls Frankie and me '*houh hoi*', little whores.

'If you don't go to sleep, I'll throw you in the river,' Ah Bing says when my mother goes out. In China, they drown unwanted girls. 'If you don't sleep, a bad man will come. Bad men like young girls like you. They don't like old ladies. What use would they have for old ladies?'

There's another threat, more oblique: 'If you don't go to sleep, I'll take you to the Chinese kitchen.' The Chinese kitchen is at the temple in Lantau. It's a long, thin room built against the bare stone of the hillside with strips of plastic roofing discoloured by mould. At night, the women chop vegetables under a bare light bulb. Strong-smelling mushrooms, ginger, thin slices of water chestnut. A dark soup boils on a kerosene burner. White squares of tofu sizzle in peanut oil. Strings of keys, plastic bags dangle on hooks. Cockroaches scuttle underfoot.

In the dark, I dream I wander through, ghostlike, looking for something. What is there here that would scare us? At the back of the kitchen, a tiger chained to the stone. The tiger is orange, whiskery like the picture on jars of tiger balm. It skulks near the wall, then whips around, lean and hungry. While the women don't see me, he does or maybe it's my scent he smells. He's waiting, ready, nostrils flared. Maybe this is the fortune Ah Sun sang for me. My punishment.

Ah Bing threatens us out of kindness. It's her way of showing affection. Of trying to guard us. She knows our parents can't look after us. Our father's away. Our mother's too naïve; she doesn't know all the bad things that can happen. It's our own fault too because we're *houh hoi*. Just being girls makes us suspect.

twenty-six

'Katie-ah, will you thread the needle for me? You have good eyes. You're a young girl. Clever girl. You can read and write. You're not a stupid old woman like me.' I sit on Ah Bing's bed, lick the thread as I've seen her do and poke it through the narrow eye.

'When I was a girl your age, my mother took me to the fortune-teller. She said when I married, my husband would die.' Looking at Ah Bing, I imagine the old fortune-teller, thin, mean, hunched with disappointments. How frightened Ah Bing must have been when the old woman snatched at her hand, forced open her white palm, stroking it with dark, gnarled fingers. The fortune-teller felt Ah Bing's disgust, her defiant nature, her wilfulness. She looked into Ah Bing's eyes and wreaked her revenge. The only way to avoid her curse is for Ah Bing to marry an old man. 'A man as old as me,' she said.

'A few years later, I was fifteen, my aunt took me to the Kuan Yin house. My aunt said, "Look at all your sisters, how hard they have to work with babies on their backs." I told my mother, "I'm not marrying, I'm staying at the Kuan Yin house." My mother was angry. She was angry with my aunt. She said I would become a hungry ghost; I would have no children to look after me, to worship me when I die.'

'Didn't you want children?' I ask.

'*Po!* Having babies is hard and sore. If you die, your spirit will sit in a pool of blood. You cannot get out until your child marries. What if your child dies? You are stuck there for ever.' Ah Bing tosses her head, incredulous of my ignorance, my naïveté. 'If your husband isn't good, your children won't be good either,' she says to prove her point, because most likely he won't be.

She stops talking, sews faster. I look down, waiting for her anger to subside, then ask how she persuaded her mother to let her go.

'My mother saw I wouldn't change my mind. She gave me thirty pounds of rice. She paid the Kuan Yin house four dollars a month for food. I had food but no clothes. I had to find a job to buy these things.'

Ah Bing smiles when she talks of her temple in China. The way she breathes in, I imagine the women laughing and teasing, the way they do at Lantau. The brief moment of quiet as they sit, start to shovel dinners of rice or congee into their mouths. The sun setting over rice paddies. 'Each morning, we woke at four to chant prayers to Kuan Yin,' Ah Bing says. 'It was my duty to clean the altar, sweep the tile floors. After these chores, I went to work. I and another girl, we travelled across the river to work at a factory making clay roof tiles. Filling wood moulds with red river mud. That was before I went to Singapore, then came here to Hong Kong.'

Ah Bing likes it when I sit and listen to her. Frankie's not interested. While Ah Bing regards my father with suspicion, she always gives me the benefit of the doubt, even if I am *houh hoi*. In the morning, she lets me light her joss sticks. I bow three times. When my mother's out, Frankie and I eat lunch with her in her back room, rice in lettuce and ginger broth, served with dried oysters, salty black beans. We laugh about my parents, her friends at the temple, the way my father refused to wear clean shirts the last time he came home. 'Men smell bad,' Ah Bing says.

'Katie-ah, you my tummy come,' she tells me. I belong to her. I'm her favourite. I'm the daughter she might have had. A girl she might have been if she'd had more chances, if she could read and write, if her mother hadn't sent her away. Ah Bing also has things I long for: the serenity of her temple, its simplicity, solitude, her independence. I want to travel across the river each day to fill wood moulds with red river mud.

twenty-seven

The deaf boy splashes up to where I am sitting at the sea's edge. The waves wash over us. It makes me uncomfortable how close he sits, the way he examines my mouth, although I know he's lip-reading. He's got something in his hand.

Smiling, he uncurls his fingers for me to see. A small purple shell. He flattens his palm, waits for the creature inside to emerge.

I wish the snail would hurry up. I wish the deaf boy would go away, swim back to the junk where our mothers sit, eating lunch. I don't want the others to see us. I don't want Frankie to make any suggestive comments. Or to notice how he pays more attention to me. The deaf boy seeks me out. I don't ask him to. He doesn't know about me. He doesn't know about the lychees.

'*Janthina globosa*, purple sea snail,' he says quietly, looking down. The snail's name, like a foreign country, a whole world, with caves and Buddha to be discovered. Its own stories.

'They live out at sea so they're unusual to find.' His voice is nasal and slurred. 'They float and feed on hydrozoa, which are like tiny jellyfish.' I look at the deaf boy's hands.

~   ~   ~

This is what I know about the deaf boy. He's Chinese. His mother is from Shanghai. His father is Cantonese. His father left because he's an artist. He couldn't paint with a baby, a deaf baby wailing, crying, throwing inarticulate tantrums. My mother says it's unusual for a Hong Kong Chinese to be a painter. The deaf boy's father paints with traditional ink and brush but his compositions are 'abstract and bold' with 'gashes and shrieks of colour', words my mother used. His paintings are different from hers. They are loud, angry, ugly, like the quarried hills of Kowloon. Hers are gentle, quiet, idyllic landscapes, bearing no signs of human destruction.

This is something else I know. The deaf boy collects shells, starfish skeletons, dried sea urchins, the chalky bone of cuttlefish. He keeps them on shelves in his room. He collects rocks, snakeskins, beetle carcasses, the brilliant blue feathers of kingfishers, broken bits of green turtle eggs he found after the villagers dug them up from Sham Wan Beach. In his room are books called *Flora Hongkongensis*, *Rambles in Hong Kong*, *Walden Pond*, *Silent Spring*. At night, he goes out, he catches snakes and frogs, geckos. He catches crickets, stick bugs, silkworms, a praying mantis. He loves animals, I think, the way my father loves the war in Vietnam.

Jen said her husband would have left anyway. Their boy being deaf only made him stay longer. She said it was her fault too. 'I couldn't look after my husband as well,' she said. I remember when she said that because it surprised me. I thought you had to take care of everyone. I didn't know you could choose. Maybe that's why my mother can't look after us. Why she's sending Frankie to boarding school. She chooses our father. She loves him more.

~　　~　　~

The snail's belly licks the deaf boy's palm, it slithers down the side of his thumb. I move my hand against his, hold still until the snail climbs across. Its dark body carries with it a spiral temple, a hiding place, a retreat, secrets. The deaf boy keeps his hands against mine. The sand swirls around the backs of our legs. Frankie swims out from the junk.

The deaf boy wants to touch me. Even if it's only the sides of our hands, the first contact between our skins, bones. If he likes me more than Frankie, it's because I'm quiet, secretive. I have to be sought out. I interest him. I'm like the snail, a foreign country. *Janthina globosa*, Saigon, Pleiku, the Mekong, Hue.

twenty-eight

Earlier that summer, my father takes us out on the junk to watch the dragon-boat races at Stanley. Each team comes from a different fishing village: Stanley, Aberdeen, Tai Tam, Po Toi. Muscular rowers churn sea and air into a frothy white. Paddles thrash as the long, slim boats skim the sea. Painted dragon-head prows leap, neck and neck, mouths open, eyes bulging, whiskers quivering. Midshipmen pound drums in rhythms like heartbeats, to urge the rowers on.

The noise will wake celestial dragons. When they fight, there will be thunder and rain needed for crops.

After lunch, my father asks Ah Wong to row us ashore in the dinghy. Frankie shoves past me as she scrambles to sit next to my father at the stern. My mother stays on board the junk to tidy the picnic.

Besides inducing rain, the races commemorate the death of Chu Yuan, a famous third-century poet who drowned himself in a river after being exiled by the emperor, my father tells us.

'When they heard the news, fishermen raced out in their boats to try to find him,' my father says. 'They scattered rice on the water as offerings. But the poet's ghost appeared to them, complaining that a greedy sea monster had eaten it all. He asked the fishermen to make special cakes, wrapped in iris leaves and tied with silk threads in five colours.'

We row through a flotilla of junks, shrouds strewn with colourful banners, lanterns and signal flags. Smoke wafts out from cooking fires where sweet-smelling feasts are being prepared on board. Sampan ladies call out, offering cut fares to ferry people ashore. Others row sightseers out for a closer view of the races. Three boys swim out and shimmy up an anchor line, the same way Frankie and I like to.

The pier is so crowded, we have to scramble across several boats moored side to side to get ashore. There's a five-tiered grandstand set up along the waterfront for important visitors. On the top tier, the statue of Tien Hou presides from her red throne. She's been carried out of her temple for the day.

Tien Hou is the fishermen's goddess. Her shrine has a place in the cabin of every Hong Kong junk. When she was only a girl in Fujian Province, she rushed down to the beach in the middle of a raging storm and, pointing to her family's fishing boat, magically guided it home.

My father photographs two lion dancers, arriving on a lighter. The huge, colourful, pug-faced head thrusts one way, then another, eyelids fluttering. He squats down to photograph children eating the special Chun Tze rice cakes and others with candied apples on sticks. He photographs the ramshackle village, men betting on dice games. He climbs to the top of bamboo scaffolding set up for a travelling night opera to get a better shot.

'Let's hope it's strong enough,' Frankie says darkly. My father says it's marvellous to photograph people celebrating for a change.

Frankie's my secret sister but not when my father is home. Late in the afternoon, we follow the winning team up into the Tien Hou temple. Inside it's so full of joss, people crushing, it's hard to breathe. My father extends his littlest finger, which is how we hold hands. But Frankie grabs hold first, draws herself close, blocking me out.

Frankie would happily leave me here, I think, among the gongs, the banners, the smoke-blackened deities, the huge coils of joss hanging from ancient wooden beams, the fearsome dragon boat's prow and tail, which are carried in behind us to be stored here for the year. Just to have him to herself.

I peer into a side room. There's a mop, a low wooden stool, a bucket with bottles of cleaning fluids, wood polish. I would like to sit there. After everyone left, the old caretaker would shuffle over. He wouldn't ask me any questions. He'd squat down, pour us tea.

He'd tell me the story of the temple bell and drum, which once belonged to the Chinese pirate Chang Pao. The story of the blackened, moth-eaten skin that hangs on the temple wall. The last tiger shot in Hong Kong, killed by Japanese soldiers just outside the temple in 1942. The story of how, when the Japanese attacked Stanley from the sea, two shells fell right into the temple grounds. Hundreds of villagers crowded here, seeking refuge. The bombs could have killed them all. But miraculously, neither exploded.

Then he'd grow quiet. We'd sit in silence, contemplating the greatness of Tien Hou, a young girl who rescued her family from a storm at sea.

~   ~   ~

Before the main altar, the triumphant rowers present Tien Hou with their prize: a glistening roast pig. Still wearing T-shirts and bandannas, sweaty from the heat, they lower the huge platter on to the altar table, nudge it between brass urns full of joss sticks, bells, wooden fish gongs, candelabras. They bow three times, knocking their heads to the floor, to thank the goddess for their luck and her patronage. Painted carvings along a screen that edges the table show Tien Hou. She rides on the back of a giant fish, pulling sailors from the sea.

twenty-nine

My father opens his suitcase on the bed. Six small packages nestle between his shirts like eggs, wrapped in newspaper with Vietnamese script. Inside are tiny lanterns, about six inches tall, made of light green glass.

My father buys some paraffin. He carries the lanterns out on to the veranda at dusk. They are the lights used in outdoor cafés in Vietnam. They remind him of Danang. They conjure quiet evenings on the beach at Nha Trang, the lull of the waves, the scratch of palm trees, the lights of Vietnamese fishing boats flickering above the dark water like fallen stars.

'Aren't they pretty, Marianne?' he asks.

My mother smiles. But I can tell the lanterns make her sad. They remind her of places she cannot see.

When my father goes back to Saigon, she pours the paraffin back into the bottle and hides the glass lanterns at the back of a bookshelf, hoping he'll forget them, forget Vietnam one day.

thirty

My father balances his camera on a tripod of driftwood, peers through the viewfinder, pulls the timed shutter release and rushes to join us.

'Keep still,' he says.

Frankie throws her arms around me. The shutter snaps. We all laugh as if it's magic. Me, Frankie, the deaf boy. Behind us, my mother, Jen, Ah Bing, Lewis and Trung. It's my birthday, August 6th. We're at Hung Shing Yeh beach on Lamma Island, near where the deaf boy lives.

For my birthday, my father gives me two books: an illustrated copy of Robert Louis Stevenson's *The Bottle Imp* and a collection of ghost stories by Guy de Maupassant. Frankie has secretly knitted me a woollen hat. It's striped with bright colours: orange, yellow, blue, green, pink.

'You can wear it when we go to America,' she says. I put it on straight away. The deaf boy gives me a tiny jade monkey, small enough to fit in the palm of my hand.

My mother makes a sachertorte, my favourite cake. She keeps it cool on ice that drips from the bottom of the rattan picnic bag. Frankie and I blow out fourteen candles, one to grow on. Sea water splashes on the chocolate icing. My mother breaks the unmelted ice and drops it into tall glasses of fresh lemonade.

Frankie teases me when I ask to invite the deaf boy. I hide the monkey in my pocket. Later, when we go to America, I tie it to a string and wear it around my neck.

~ ~ ~

That evening I sit out on the veranda on a large pillow that covers a rattan chair. It's dusk. Already, two sampans are out fishing the rocky peninsula below. One carries a bright light. From the other, you can hear the sound of knocking. The light and noise lure fish into a net stretched between them.

From inside, I hear my father's chair scrape back from the table where he's been reading the newspapers. I tuck my feet under me. If you come out now, I urge him silently, if you come outside, where no one else can hear us, I will tell you everything. I will tell you about the butcher shop, the men from Lantau, the explosion. What happened to Frankie and me.

My father walks out through the French doors holding his camera. He squats close, looks at me through the viewfinder, focuses. I stare straight into the lens. I am sunburned from the beach. Flushed with anticipation. My heart begins to beat wildly. I lean forward.

When my father puts the camera down, I will speak. If I can just say Dad, the rest will come. Dad, a woman died, a boy was burned. Dad, I don't know what the men did to Frankie. Dad, help me. Then whatever happens next won't matter. He'll look after us. I won't have to think about the lychees any more.

The shutter clicks.

'Kate, don't look so serious.' My father peers at me around the camera. My eyes begin to smart. My throat constricts. It's the chance I've been waiting for. I am thirteen.

'Dad?' I say.

But just then, Frankie bounds out. She must have seen us through the glass doors. My father kneeling down so close. Me, about to reveal our secrets, confess our sins. Doesn't she want me to help her?

'Dad!' Frankie yelps. Leaping on to his back, she twines her arms around his neck, rubs her soft cheek against the scratchy stubble of his face, like a cat.

'Hold on, Frankie,' my father barks. His voice uncharacteristically sharp as if he knows I have something to tell him. Frankie drops her hands. It's not the response she expected. Abjectly, she fondles the camera that hangs around his neck.

'Frankie, you'll just have to wait.' My father starts to rise from his knees, to straighten his back. But Frankie's quick. She won't be put off. Before he can stand, she runs her thumbs around the side of his camera and pushes the button that releases the back, exposing his film.

Bringing up his arms, my father throws Frankie off so that she stumbles backwards. 'Now why in heaven's name would you do that?' he snarls. Frankie shrugs, looks sullenly at me, as if it's my fault. Secret sisters.

'Marianne!' my father bellows. Snapping his camera shut, he winds in the film, extracts the roll and buttons it safely in his shirt pocket – away from Frankie.

'Marianne!' he shouts.

'It's all right,' my mother reassures, trying to smooth things over. 'Only the last shots will be ruined. The others will be fine.' I look down, finger the books my father gave me, *The Bottle Imp* and ghost stories by Guy de Maupassant. I try not to cry. My mother thinks I'm upset about the film, the photographs of my birthday. She doesn't know what I want to tell, a revelation that could have changed everything, saved Frankie.

But most likely, I wouldn't have been able to say anything. Just as I don't say anything now. And maybe, he couldn't have helped us anyway.

~   ~   ~

The next morning at breakfast, my father gives me a present, a photograph, one he stayed up late to develop even though he's leaving for Saigon. It's the one on the junk, me in Frankie's hat, with Frankie's arms around me.

thirty-one

Kuan Yin is the Goddess of Mercy, the Virgin Bodhisattva. Like Ah Bing, Kuan Yin refused to marry. She was a princess who rejected riches and marriage in order to live the life of a hermit. She was a holy person who could have reached nirvana, enlightenment, but stepped back because she heard the cries of the world.

'I am Kuan Yin. I won't eat meat and I won't marry!' Ah Bing recites Kuan Yin's vows. If you don't eat meat, your blood will be weak, her parents told her. If you don't have children, you'll be a hungry ghost.

Kuan Yin's father was so enraged he sent his soldiers to her temple to burn it down, but the fire would not burn. He sent executioners with swords to kill her, but the swords broke in their hands. Finally, he gave in. He worshipped her, a mere girl. She became a great goddess, more loved than Buddha himself.

From Hsiang Shan, the temple of immortals, on Putuo Island, Kuan Yin heard news of her father's illness: horrible ulcers covered his body so he could not sleep day or night. She instructed the king's messengers to gouge out her left eye, cut off her left hand. Only a remedy made from these ingredients would cure him. When the messengers returned to the king's palace, Kuan Yin's mother recognized a black scar on her daughter's hand.

Kuan Yin hears the world's cries, the cries of the poor and the hungry, the orphaned, the maimed, the napalmed. Invoked by mothers in childbirth, by unmarried daughters, by nuns. Ah Bing's mentor, her saint, her saviour. She comes down from heaven like Jesus, performs miracles, heals the burned boy's scars.

When Kuan Yin told Ah Bing to leave her missee's house in Singapore, it was not the only time the goddess saved her. The goddess also came to the Coolie House, a workers' hostel, where Ah Bing stayed when she first came to Hong Kong after the Japanese left. Ah Bing lay sick on the straw mat she rented for a bed.

'Aya, Kate, my legs were swollen as wide as watermelons,' Ah Bing says. 'I talked like a crazy person. Then Kuan Yin floated into the room. She floated in midair. She wore a blue dress. She was the size of a teacup. "Get up," Kuan Yin ordered. "How can I?" I asked. "I think I will die." "Sit up," Kuan Yin said. After that, I got better.'

~   ~   ~

I'm alone in Ah Bing's room. My mother and Frankie have gone out to buy some clothes for boarding school. My father's gone back to Saigon. Ah Bing's on the back patio, sweeping. I stand in front of the Kuan Yin altar. I light three joss sticks. Holding them in my hands, I bow three times.

Ah Bing's Kuan Yin is a diminutive white porcelain statuette, only eight inches high. Not as regal, or as forbidding, as the polished wood statue at Lantau. Fragile, dainty, she sits behind a soup tin full of burned joss, a chipped bowl of waxy oranges piled in a pyramid, a plate of longans, three hard candies individually wrapped in colourful paper, left as offerings.

Can you help me, Kuan Yin? Can you protect me from dead bodies floating up in the sea; from the Viet Cong hiding in the hills; from my body changing; from the lychees I carried; from Frankie?

Kuan Yin is dressed in flowing robes, she floats on a porcelain lotus flower. She clasps her hands resignedly in her lap, one over the other. Cross-legged. Serene. Her eyes look downward, hooded, contemplative. Like Ah Bing, Kuan Yin's face is wide and comforting. She wears her hair in a simple bun on top of her head. But her tiny features, her pouty lips painted red, betray a quiet sensuality. It's not just her altruism, I think, but her own earthly love that keeps her here.

thirty-two

In his room, the deaf boy asks if he can kiss me. Sea water from my bathing suit runs down the back of my legs, drips on to the floor. We're both standing. My back flattens against the wall. My bare shoulder scratches against a cobra skin.

Outside I hear sounds he cannot hear: flip-flops passing on the cement path, mahjong pieces clattering from the house next door, the chatter of women cooking.

'Ginger, hot pepper oil, garlic, sesame,' the deaf boy picks out these smells. His voice warbles. 'Jasmine, joss, sea salt, Kate's skin.'

The deaf boy can only see, smell, touch, taste. He runs his hands over my bony shoulders, the sharp points of my elbows, shyly across my childish breasts, pointy, hard and damp under my wet bathing suit.

When I close my eyes, I hear the chop of a Huey lifting off, the distant thud of mortar. I wonder what the women next door think when they see us come in, Jen's deaf boy and a *gwaimui*, white ghost girl. The deaf boy sees me listening, listening for the others who will soon arrive, back from the beach where we've been swimming.

Kissing the deaf boy is like tasting the sea. It's like forgiveness. His mouth is dark and salty and wet. It licks and sucks. Unable to breathe, I pull away.

~   ~   ~

If he stays quiet, doesn't move, I'll lick the salt off his cheeks, his eyes, his eyebrows, his nose, his lips. Quiet, without moving. I'll pretend we're in the jungle, its triple canopy, along the Ho Chi Minh Trail. Leeches bleed our legs. Phosphorus glows in rotting vegetation. There are tigers here. Don't make a sound. I'll lick him until he kisses me again. I love the deaf boy. I think of nothing else.

Thirty-three

Frankie doesn't want to go to Miss Tipley's party, but my mother insists. Miss Tipley's sister is visiting from London and she has a son in his first year at Cambridge. It would be nice for him to meet us.

Frankie protests with fingernail polish and mascara she stole from the Lane Crawford department store. Naked, she props her toes on the bed and leans over to paint them. Her neck stretches long. When the polish dries, she dresses in her Indian print skirt, ties the ends of her shirt provocatively to show her belly. My mother doesn't say anything. In a fortnight, Frankie will go to boarding school. The colour Frankie stole is nice, a milky lavender.

~   ~   ~

Miss Tipley's nephew's name is George. He wears a suit. He's got an accent like the BBC World Service, though he's only eighteen. He welcomes us into the front hall as if it were his house, not Marjorie's, as if we were the visitors, not him.

'You lookee Ah Mei? Ah Mei back room, kitchen,' he informs Ah Bing, in BBC pidgin. Ah Bing could find her way without his help. Even worse is his smug grin, as if, in his few days here, he's mastered a foreign language. He already knows how to keep the natives in order. Frankie sniggers behind his back.

'Hello, hello,' Miss Tipley says, panting slightly as she comes up the stairs. *'Jousan, Bing-ah, neih hou ma?'* Hello, Ah Bing, how are you?

'Hou hou.' Ah Bing hurries away, suddenly self-conscious among the dressed-up foreigners, the BBC. George puts his arm around his mother, gives her shoulders a proprietary squeeze.

'When I opened my handbag at the airport, we thought Fifi was dead, didn't we?' George's mother says. Her voice is high, piercing, her question aimed at the tiny dog she holds in her arm. 'I think I might have gone a little overboard with the sedative.' Her laugh is nervous and too loud, as if it is directed through people not at them.

'George, darling, would you get me a top-up?' She wears a short red silk skirt with matching top and pearls. Behind her, on a chair in the corner of the hall, is a mannequin of a woman, completely naked.

Miss Tipley's sister is not at all like her. Penelope wears black baggy trousers like an amah. She ties her greying hair loosely back with a simple tortoiseshell clip. Penelope looks like a man, while her sister's excessively female. It's as if they've set themselves off, one against the other.

Back with his mother's drink, George notices Frankie touching the mannequin.

'They were throwing her out at the Daimaru department store so I bought her for my aunt. I thought she'd appreciate it.' He raises one eyebrow and looks at Miss Tipley suggestively. It's as if he broadcasts our taboo. Shouts, Miss Tipley's *mo daofu*, she kisses Miss Innis. I feel my mother shrink.

'Come, let's go out to the garden,' Miss Tipley says, ignoring

George. Because the house is built on a steep hill, you have to go down a flight of stairs, past the bedrooms.

Outside, the garden's lit with coloured lanterns that stretch down towards the pool. I hear the formal, consonant-filled tones of Mandarin, the rapid, lively staccato of Cantonese, a woman arguing heatedly in French. At the far end, near the pool house, a small record player churns out rock-and-roll. Waiters in black suits bring drinks. Below us the dark, jungled hillside drops down towards the city with its strings of lights. Boats dart back and forth across the harbour like lighted water bugs.

We follow Miss Tipley. George is still talking. Like his mother, he's loud but his voice is self-assured while hers is flighty, almost helpless. It's hard to believe he's just a few years older than us. I've never met a boy who wears a suit, brings drinks, has his own money to spend. If Frankie and I wanted that mannequin, we'd have to steal it. It doesn't seem George needs to meet anyone or ask anything. He has nothing to find out.

Frankie saunters directly to the pool as if we've come for a swim, takes off her sandals, and sits dangling her legs in the warm water. She pulls her skirt high up her thighs. I sit down next to her, unsure whether to take off my own shoes or not. Ah Pak, Miss Tipley's driver, dressed tonight in a black suit, offers us juice. Frankie takes two glasses of wine instead and Ah Pak giggles.

'If her dog had died, Miss Tipley's sister could have worn it over her shoulder,' Frankie sneers. 'She's half-gone herself. I wonder if she uses the dog's sedatives.' I laugh. In this way, we reassert our world. Sirens of the pool. It's the others who are strange, awkward, misplaced, not us.

'Here comes George,' I say.

'Shall we ask him for a top-up?' Frankie laughs.

It's impressive how she manipulates George. He scurries off to get her another glass of wine. She tells him what records to play. The Rolling Stones, The Doors, records my father listens to when he's back from Vietnam. Frankie acts as if they're hers. When George talks dismissively about Cambridge, Frankie pours contempt on her future school in Massachusetts. 'It's my grandmother's old school,' she says. I never heard that before.

I want to tell Frankie to stop. It's not worth impressing this boy. Despite her scorn, she flirts with George, seduced by her own exaggerations, her lies, her brown thighs, her needs.

You don't need George, I want to tell her. You don't need him or Humphries or Pym. Can't you see, we'll survive on our own? We've got the clothes under Ah Bing's bed. We've got our shacks of flotsam and jetsam. We're secret sisters. We don't need a father. We don't need to tell anyone anything.

The record whines – a Doors song about setting the night on f-i-r-e. That's a Vietnam song, not yours, I want to tell Frankie. It's about napalm, not sex. Frankie pulls her skirt higher up her thighs. She wraps George around her neck like a dead dog. I can't stop her from doing what she wants.

~   ~   ~

In the kitchen, Ah Bing smiles at me with her gold teeth. Ah Mei shoves tidbits my way. I'm safe here, an honoured guest, coddled by familiar sounds of scraping dishes, clattering silverware, Ah Bing and Ah Mei teasing, confiding in Cantonese. The Chinese kitchen is safe, my temple. The tiger I imagine when Ah Bing threatens us at night is not here. Perhaps he's been let free, he's outside roaming. I feel him crouching behind my mother when she comes to the door.

'Could you run and find Frankie? It's time to go home.'

I go down the stairs, turn inward towards the bedrooms, not the garden. I hear George's mother in the hallway upstairs. 'Oh that obscene mannequin. When I woke up yesterday morning, I saw it lying under the piano. I thought, good heavens, what has George done to some poor girl now?' George said they were going to find more records.

The hallway is white with rush matting. Along the walls are nineteenth-century prints of the foreign factories at Canton, each flying its own flag: British, French, Dutch, American. I put my ear to the closed door. I don't know whether to knock. I'd rather not make a noise.

'You can wait here if you want, make sure no one comes,' Frankie had said as she shut the door and shut me out. I shook my head.

I turn the handle slowly until it stops, then gently push the door open, just a fraction, just enough to see into the gloom. The curtains are drawn. Inside, I see Frankie. She's flattened on the bed, her skirt pulled all the way up now. Above her, George's large white bottom. His trousers are pulled down to his knees. He's shed his shoes but he still has his socks on.

Frankie's head whips around. I think she's been crying; her mascara's smudged, her shirt's untied. She looks small, crushed beneath George's large body. She glares at the door, open just a fraction, not enough to see out. George grunts, noticing nothing. I shut the door quickly, slowly release the handle, letting the catch slip silently into its groove.

A few minutes later, when Frankie comes upstairs, she's washed her face. She's tied her shirt. She looks calm, defiant. How could my mother ever know she's *houh hoi*? How could she know about the bomb, the butcher shop? We disguise ourselves so well.

'We have to go,' I say apologetically. Before we can escape, George strides into the room, gives Frankie's shoulders a too familiar squeeze, like the one he gave his mother earlier. I see Frankie hates him for that. He could give her away. Expose her. He keeps no secrets. On the drive home, Frankie is silent, sullen. Ah Bing chatters in the front seat. '*Aiyah*, Ah Mei gave me too much food, too many leftovers.' She pats the basket at her feet contentedly.

'He seemed like such a nice boy, Miss Tipley's nephew,' my mother says.

thirty-four

Fucked is the word Frankie uses. Fucked George. She says it coarsely, implying the metaphorical sense of the word. She had sex but, more importantly, she hurt him, beat him, conquered him. She left him scarred, damaged for life. I'd like to believe her. I'm sure she's capable of it. But I also know what I saw.

No, I want to shout at her. I saw you crying. Your make-up was smudged. You looked squashed. I saw George squeeze your shoulder, put you in your place. You're as pathetic as his mother, as her little dog Fifi.

To my surprise, I wish Frankie had fucked Humphries instead. Humphries would have been kinder, more gentle. Why George? I don't want to be secret sisters if what you tell me is lies. If you never ask me about the lychees. I don't want to be asked to see things the way you want me to, it's not true. I don't want to be doorkeeper for you and George.

'It'll teach her to make me go to parties,' Frankie says. That Frankie seduced George, had sex with him, for revenge, shocks me. Now I see, it's not the pudgy man she's after, it's not Humphries, it's my mother, it's me. She hates my mother for wanting her to be different than she is. She hates me for keeping her secrets, for being her confidante, her alibi, her sister, without being able to help her or protect her. I am too young.

If my mother forces her to meet nice boys, she'll pull up her skirt, take down their trousers.

~ ~ ~

'So now you can tell me if you did it with Fish,' Frankie demands.

'Did what?' I ask, dissembling.

'You know, fuck him.'

'Don't be stupid. I don't even like Fish. He's deaf.'

'Being deaf doesn't mean he can't do it,' Frankie taunts.

It's like this for Frankie. A race, a competition, a dare. Who will do it first? Who loves who more? Is it my fault she fucked George? Was she worried I'd already gone first?

More crucial, do we love Frankie? Do we love her enough? Can we? Do I? Does my father? My mother? She isn't sure. That's why she boasts, throws herself at men: George, my father's friends. That's why she runs after Red Guards. She wants to see if we can stop her.

If the deaf boy swims over to me, if my father sits too close to me on the junk, I betray her. I shouldn't allow it. I should disappear, let her go first. Frankie has to be careful now, vigilant because she knows what I've done, what I'm capable of. She has to keep a constant lookout in case I usurp her position, switch my allegiance, desert her. In case I am more loved.

I'm Kate, *muimui*, little sister. I'm not supposed to have my own secrets, my own needs, my own desires. I'm supposed to be swamped with hers. There's not enough room for both of us.

I don't want to be awed by Frankie any more. I don't want to be the fine weight on the balance board that keeps Frankie from toppling over. Quietly, without warning, I step off.

thirty-five

I go to the deaf boy's house. It is dark, shady, with lacquered wood floors, high bookshelves. Coloured silk pillows glint from low benches. A ceiling fan throbs overhead. It is dark but when I step forward a sharp ray of sunlight pierces through a high window, blinds me. I can't see. But I feel my own face lit up, white, scared, exposed.

The deaf boy takes my hand and pulls me gently forward into the dark. Our wet feet leave silvery footprints on the black floor, up the stairs, glinting like fish scales.

The deaf boy lays me on his bed. Unwraps me slowly, the way I've watched him pry a starfish from a rock. Kneeling beside me, he slips my bathing suit top over my arms, my head, exposing my small breasts. He pulls the pants down over my gangly legs, revealing a blonde triangle of hair, my white skin.

Naked, I lie completely still. Close my eyes. I pretend I am an object he carried in from the beach. A bone washed up, a sun-bleached cuttlefish, a ridged cowrie shell. I am thin, hard. I am not voluptuous. I am a rock with edges, unsmoothed. White quartz, veins of dark obsidian where the rattan shade casts lines of sun and shadow across the bed.

The deaf boy examines my naked body. He runs his hands slowly over me from my mouth down to my navel, as if I were a shell, *Janthina globosa*. He runs his fingers between my legs, feels where it is wet, trails the wetness down my thighs, exploring. I feel my breath become fast and short. I grow full of desire. Desire for the deaf boy's kisses, for death, for drowning. Outside the village sounds are muted, far away. It's midday, too hot to work.

I undress the deaf boy. I do the things he has done to me. I lie him down and touch him until he moans with pleasure. I lick him. The deaf boy's skin is smooth, salty. I trace the lines of his ribs and collar-bone with my tongue. We touch each other this way, nothing more. Then we lie down, we don't speak, don't move.

thirty-six

When my father goes out on a mission, he flies in a MedEvac helicopter. It's empty on the way out, it's going to pick up the wounded. On the way back, he catches a ride with a resupply helicopter that's delivered its load. The Viet Cong carry their rice and guns and medicine hundreds of miles through the mountainous jungles along the Ho Chi Minh Trail. They carry their wounded to makeshift underground hospitals. The Americans fly in beer and spare ribs for the Fourth of July. Also Coca-Cola, soap, shaving cream, cigarettes, chewing gum. These luxuries don't make it any easier to be shot at, kill, watch someone die.

Flying, though, puts you above it. It gives a distance that makes you feel you know the country, understand it in a way you don't always on the ground. The helicopters are huge, ungainly, *great iron birds*, the Viet Cong call them, but from up high you see the whole country. The blue mountains of the Annamite Cordillera, the sea, the rice paddies, green as a parrot's wing. You smell the smoke of charcoal cooking fires, burnt sugar, jasmine flowers. It's luscious. The door of the helicopter is open. The wind is hot. It makes you want to laugh, you're so lucky. Cry, because you have a deep sense of longing, nostalgia. It feels as if you're a boy again. It feels like love.

Then you look down, more carefully. You hold your breath. What's there? Burned villages, blackened jungle, palm trees blown out of the ground. Families hide at the entrance to a tunnel. A frightened water buffalo careens down the beach. Craters everywhere.

Small three-foot craters blasted out by artillery fire. Star-shaped craters, the work of anti-personnel bombs. Forty-foot holes left by delayed-fuse bombs. Worst of all, the mile-long lines of huge thirty-foot craters running through fields, up mountains. Blown out by pay-loads of six-hundred-pound bombs, dropped from 40,000 feet in the air by the Arc Lights, the B-52s. My father can identify them all.

I imagine looking down, the deafening chop chop of the helicopter blades. If I close my eyes, I see a dead body floating up from the sea. I see my sister. I see Lantau. 'Don't look down,' my mother says. 'Don't look at what she's doing now. Don't look at the Red Guards.'

~   ~   ~

Once my father hitched a ride back to Danang. The helicopter was ready to leave when the Marine captain decided to load it with bodies. His unit had run out of body bags so the men wrapped the dead in ponchos. The helicopter took off with the door open. Even so the stench was awful. Then the wind pulled the ponchos off. When my father looked around him, he saw dead faces, blown-apart faces, faces that had turned black in the heat. Blood and mucus flew out from under the ponchos, splattering his clothes, his face. At a thousand feet, my father wanted to jump out. That was the worst he'd seen, the closest he'd come.

thirty-seven

It's the end of summer, Frankie's last week in Hong Kong, before my mother will take her to boarding school. My father is coming back from Vietnam to put them on the plane. Only he hasn't arrived yet. We crowd on to the small, half-eroded rock pier like sea birds drying their wings, waiting for Ah Wong to row in. He makes several trips back and forth from the anchored junk.

I help load the picnic baskets into the dinghy. Frankie wears her cut-off shorts, a shirt that shows her belly button with a silver chain around her middle. Where did she get it?

It's still, humid, hazy. The rocky coast smells damp, overripe, seaweed stews in the sun. Nevertheless, I wear one of Ah Bing's lumpy green sweaters, knitted with leftover yarn, large buttons and pockets in the front. I am cold. I wait for Ah Wong's last trip in case my father arrives. I look for him in the dark shadows of banyans that line the road, tiny altars tucked among their roots.

'He might have missed the plane or it might just be late,' Pym says kindly. 'Anyway, we'll leave the motorboat for him, in case he makes it.' The motorboat's a fast, two-hundred-horsepower outboard that belongs to Pym; sometimes he takes us water-skiing. He swings the last rattan bag into the dinghy and waits for me to climb in. I trail my fingers in the water, watch the ripples they make, look back into the trees once more. Pym's boat left tied to the pier.

My father might be dead. Maybe the Viet Cong got him after all. If he doesn't come, Frankie won't be able to say goodbye. He won't be able to fix things before she goes. Pray to Kuan Yin.

My mother doesn't say anything. She busies herself with the bags. It's our last picnic of the summer. She's invited my father's friends. When my mother returns from America, she'll come back without Frankie. I'll be at school here, the Prisoner of War School. She'll busy herself with her painting. Maybe she'll stop being scared of what Frankie will do. Maybe she'll change her mind, let Frankie stay. It's just that Frankie has grown so wild, so unruly, she said. She said she doesn't know how to be Frankie's mother. Maybe she's just worrying about my father.

We set off without him, even though Frankie swings angrily off the awning poles, hanging out over the water, scowling. Bare feet, bare arms, bare middle. He's deserted her again.

We anchor at Middle Bay, which is just around the headland, a pretty beach fronting green jungle. Concrete steps and a railing descend from Repulse Bay Road. We'll wait here, have our picnic. Later, we'll head off to Lamma or Po Toi, one of the outlying islands. If my father comes, he'll bring with him the excitement, the contagious adrenalin of war. Then, we'll be Marco Polo, Cortez, Cook, surveying, mapping, exploring. We'll walk through villages, seek out wrinkled women who dry fish in rattan baskets and stand off mangy dogs that run at us, teeth bared. We'll be Viet Cong, keep to the shadows, walk noiselessly past bombed houses in rubber sandals. My father will camouflage our helmets with leaves.

~   ~   ~

Middle Bay is already full of bathers. Young couples splash out to a bathing float. Families congregate in cool circles of shade cast by elephant ear trees, dark circles on white sand. They lay out picnics. At the back of the beach, a huge banyan sends tangles of roots into the earth. There is a white, concrete boathouse where skiffs are kept. A small shop sells red bean ice-cream and cold chrysanthemum tea. A lifeguard perched in his high tower wears a red-and-yellow bathing suit and a whistle around his neck. A white triangular flag flutters in the breeze, showing it's safe to swim.

My mother unpacks the picnic, lays out her wares on colourful cloths spread along the deck: cold cucumber soup, barbecued ribs wrapped in tinfoil, freshly cut French bread, lemon bars, chocolate cake, bottles of wine, a canteen of hot jasmine tea, salt and pepper shakers. These are things that help her keep going: order, perfection, colour. Even if my father's not there. Her own prettiness. Her picnics as picturesque as her paintings.

Humphries is here too, with a new girlfriend. At the bow, Pym talks earnestly to High Auntie. Frankie ignores them, glaring at the water. Perhaps these are other reasons she's angry: the secret sister perch usurped, Humphries off-limits, although I think he's only trying to protect himself from Frankie. Pym pours wine for the grown-ups. Humphries wraps his arms around his girlfriend's waist, holding her closer than my mother would like.

Then we hear it. The whine of a motorboat heading across the bay. An outboard, a boat with a single figure at the back.

'Daddy!' Frankie shouts. She stands up on the railing waving her arms. Waving as if he's coming for her only and no one else. There's no one else alive. She'll make a performance as grand as his. My mother picks Frankie's plate off the railing before it topples. My sister's showiness makes her uncomfortable. Already she doesn't like the way Frankie will jump all over my father, hang off him, demand his attention and everyone else's. It's something she doesn't let herself do. She keeps her claims quiet.

Later, Humphries told me he'd felt sorry for my mother at that moment. 'She hadn't seen your father for five, maybe six weeks. Her face lit up when she saw him coming. She was in love with him,' Humphries explained. 'But there was Frankie making all the noise, demanding to come first.'

I'm smiling though because I see it really is him and he's coming in, fast, dramatically. I can see he's grinning now, waving back. Steering the boat with just one hand. His dark hair blows back in the wind. His khaki shirt billows off his thin shoulders. As he draws nearer, I see thick stubble on his face, the beginning of the beard he is always threatening to grow.

I want my father home. I want him to take care of Frankie, to make her happy. To make my mother stop worrying. I want him to make it all right for Frankie to go to boarding school, or maybe to let her stay. To make her stop punishing us, hurting herself. I will give Frankie to him. I will tell him I can't look after her any more.

Then without warning, without looking back, Frankie jumps. She leaps off the railing, jumps into the air. I don't know whether she means to or whether she's just so carried away she can't stop herself. She must get to him first. Make him love her most. Save me, Daddy. Catch me. Take me with you.

The boat's too close, speeding neatly in. 'Frankie!' my mother shouts. My father shoves the throttle hard into reverse. But the shift's too abrupt. The outboard strains, bucks up. Frankie's falling. The boat hits Frankie with a loud thump. Then everything goes silent.

I watch my father silently scramble across the boat to reach her, to pull my sister from the sea. Frankie's slack body soaks my father's shirt. The blood from her head runs red all over the boat.

Swiftly, my father lays Frankie down across the bow of the motorboat. He puts his mouth on hers, kisses her, trying to suck the sea water from her lungs. His brown arms pump her chest but it only makes more blood come out. Pym clambers down to help him, throws the painter to Humphries to tie it down. High Auntie brings up towels. I think she wants to clean the blood off Frankie. On the beach, the lifeguard swings down from his perch, bathers stand to stare.

I see my father. I see him swear, cry out. I see in his eyes a look of ruin. Still I hear nothing. It's completely silent, except I'm screaming. It's a sound I didn't make when the body floated up, when the pudgy man pushed Frankie up against the hot tin, when the lychees exploded killing the old woman, burning the boy. It rises out of me; Frankie's cry. I don't think it will ever stop.

Far away, I feel my mother, who never holds us. She is pulling my body to hers, cradling me in her arms. The way my father cradles Frankie now, no longer trying to make her breathe. My mother doesn't ask me to stop. She doesn't tell me not to look. She holds me close against her weeping body. I think I might fly away.

thirty-eight

What can you give me?

Can you give me the sound of funereal wailing by white-clad women from a back-alley temple? The single chime of a high-pitched bell, the knocking of a wooden fish?

Can you give me the translucent green of sun shining through elephant ear leaves? The heat, the heavy rain? Can you give me the smells inside a hot teak cupboard, dried oysters, clove hair oil, joss, tiger balm, steamed rice? The smell of wet cement, rattan baskets? The sound of jackhammers?

Can you give me a handful of coloured silk? An empty pack of cigarettes? A tape recorder? A smooth stone rounded by the sea? A bone of cuttlefish? A ripened pomelo split open?

Can you give me my father's hand in mine? Frankie's in the other? Then take everything and go away?

~   ~   ~

That night I dream of blue swallowtail butterflies. They hover in the air like a kaleidoscope, alight on my body, drinking sweat from my skin. In the twilight, the Viet Cong sit around a wet fire. They lean their guns up against the feet of a huge stone Buddha. The ones who still have them take off their rubber sandals, massage their sore, bitten, feet. Frankie's feet are smooth and clean. The others look at her amazed. How did she manage it, walking barefoot through the jungle? I laugh at them. Don't they know she's a ghost?

thirty-nine

Soon we will leave Hong Kong. In our kitchen, men wrap each plate, each bowl in sheets of Chinese newspaper, stack them, tie the stacks and pack them in boxes, like ammunition for the war. It's an art, the way they work, so quick, so neat. If you look again, they might be gone, carry all our belongings down the Ho Chi Minh Trail.

My mother calls the place we're going home. I don't. Neither does my father. Our blood cries out for the tangled, dripping vines of the jungle, trees, elephant ear leaves. Its orange earth, muddy now because the rain has finally come.

My mother takes charge. She arranges everything, the packing, the airplanes that will take us away, Frankie's funeral. She looks after my father, massages his hands, his face, brings him blankets, hot tea. She is strong and able. Who would have thought it? There is no one to thwart her.

My father shivers in the heat. He swathes himself in sweaters, drapes a blanket around him, wears it like a coloured robe as he moves around the house. 'It's so cold,' he says. 'Don't you feel cold, Katenick?' If I stumble, he pulls me up quick. He's shaking with fright. When my mother cuts her finger with a kitchen knife, he weeps like a baby. During Frankie's funeral service, my mother has to lead him out of St John's. He says he'll walk up and see the animals in the Botanical Gardens. My mother asks me to go with him. We look at the green and red parrots, pink flamingos, the lone black panther pacing his cement rocks, the gibbons from Sumatra. I wonder what would happen if we set them free like General Maltby's white cockatoos.

I tell my father I would like to hear gibbons howl in the jungle. I would like to watch Viet Cong pass silently through the shadows of a leafy village without making a sound. I tell him it's a better funeral for Frankie up here with the animals. I think it's too late now to ever tell him about Lantau, the lychees.

'If you're happy here, why wasn't Frankie?' my father asks.

~   ~   ~

The war in Vietnam goes on without him. Enemy engagements. Helicopter blades. Night patrols in phosphorescent jungle. The war he loved. His country. At the end of the year, the Tet offensive, the big story, the beginning of the end. Viet Cong commandos penetrate the centre of Saigon, forcing their way into the concrete, sandbagged American Embassy. There is fighting in Nha Trang, Danang, Pleiku, Khesanh, Hue, all the places he knows. Especially Hue, where the Viet Cong fire rockets and machine guns down from the massively thick walls of the citadel of Nguyen emperors. My father's heartbroken for it. He longs for the rose-brick palaces along the Perfume River. But his body rebels. Because now he can't stand the sight of blood. He can't stand loud noises. Helicopters, motors revving make him cower like a dog. At night, he shouts out.

Ah Bing mocks my father behind his back, the same way she mocks my asthma, breathing roughly in and out. Hardships are to be endured, then left behind.

'There are other stories. Other places,' McKenna tells him the evening after Frankie's funeral. 'When this is all over, when you're ready, we'll find another place for you. Rome. Paris. London. Wherever you want.'

My father wants Vietnam. He wants Frankie. He wants to be able to reverse the motorboat in time. He wants the dead to come back to life.

forty

'Frankie will be a naughty ghost,' Ah Bing says. 'Just like she was a naughty girl. Always upsetting your mother, running off, leaving her shirt open like *houh hoi.*'

That's what the *taitais* are worried about. It's why they're so bossy, leaning over the top balcony, clucking their approval, telling Ah Bing what to do as she lights a small fire down on the front patio. They're hoping she'll be able to soothe Frankie's ghost, keep her at bay.

Ah Bing sets out a bowl of rice, a plate of oranges, some buns with red bean paste, a small cup of tea for the hungry ghosts who, at the end of each summer, are let out of hell to wander the earth. When she lights her joss sticks and prays, the food multiplies until there is enough for all. Like Jesus with the loaves and fishes.

'You have to feed them,' Ah Bing tells me. 'Give them presents so they don't make trouble.'

Americans don't know what to do with the dead. A Chinese funeral service is better. You have to wail, cry, shout out. You need musicians to clang cymbals, blow flutes to send the spirit on its way.

She feeds the flames with piles of tiny paper jackets, cutout watches, spirit-money of $100,000 notes printed with the

Chinese characters for Bank of Hell. I watch her poke each object down into the fire with a stick. The painted paper is cheap and doesn't burn well. Small sparks leap into the air. Bits of blackened banknotes drift across the garden. This morning, my mother asked her to come to America with us.

~ ~ ~

I would like to burn presents for Frankie. I would send her small coloured scarves, miniature packages of chewing gum, cigarettes boxes, Coca-Cola, television programmes from America, lavender fingernail polish. I would send her rice cakes wrapped in iris leaves, tied with silk threads of five colours. But there are too many ghosts. They drift up over the misty headland from the sea, skulk through the garden. They collect in the dark, mouldy corners of the low cement wall, brush by the house like blown leaves or thin plastic bags, charred paper. Lost, unhappy ghosts. Spirits of people who died suddenly, violently, inauspiciously. Unmarried women. Dead children. Murdered. Drowned. Ghosts without descendants to worship them. Some of the ghosts wail like babies. Others are angry, dangerous, seeking revenge. I see the drowned woman, her hair floating around her, her eye-sockets full of fish. An old woman without teeth.

~ ~ ~

When Ah Bing was a girl, her mother said she would become a hungry ghost. She'd wished that the miracle of the food multiplying would really happen so there would be a red bean bun for her too, not just for her no-good brothers Opium Kuan and Opium Dum.

'Jumping off the boat. How careless!' Ah Bing would like to scold Frankie for that. For making our family suffer. For making us leave Hong Kong too. Unless, of course, it was on purpose.

In China, it is honourable for girls to kill themselves if, for instance, they have sworn to follow Kuan Yin and then are forced into marriage, or their husbands beat them, or their in-laws make their life too hard, Ah Bing says. But if Frankie killed herself, what was it for? '*Pak tuali!* American girls too much spoiled.' Frankie always had enough food. She could read. She was about to go to a good school in America. 'American girls have everything. *Po!* Bad things happen, even in rich families.' Best to feed her now. Pray to Kuan Yin to look after her. Even naughty children need looking after.

'*Aiyah*, Katie, ghosts very happy today. Plenty money. Plenty food.' She tosses me a bun the ghosts have already eaten. 'Frankie likes this one,' Ah Bing says. The bun is thick and glutinous. It sticks to the roof of my mouth.

Out at sea, it's milky green, the colour of a lucky jade bracelet. A fishing boat chugs past heading out to deep water, its trawling booms extended so it looks like a giant bug. The fishermen feed the hungry ghosts too. They set paper boats afloat in the harbour and at the entrances to typhoon shelters.

forty-one

I think of it over and over. Frankie jumping, the thud of the boat hitting her. I hear myself scream. Sometimes I play it differently. I reach out and catch her. I hold her over the side of the boat, drop her into my father's arms. My father reverses the engine in time. He hits Frankie, she is paralysed. I take care of her for the rest of my life.

Sometimes I look at my father and he's seeing the same things. Then I want to smack Frankie. I want to spit her name like Ah Bing. *Houh hoi! Ham ga chang!* I want to push her up against the dead pig, the burning metal of the butcher shop until she cries, begs me for forgiveness. It's not just about you, I want to tell her. Then I would take my father's hand, sit down with him on the temple patio, tell him it's all right. It wasn't his fault.

Other times, I just let Frankie go. Up she floats, her freckled face grins wildly down at me until she's a mere speck. I can see she's delighted. I rejoice with her. She's jumping free. For a single moment, I see her suspended in the air above me, for ever. Sometimes I confuse the two events in my mind. It's the bomb that killed Frankie. She died in the butcher shop after all, blown up by lychees.

It's inevitable, Frankie's death. The result of carefully laid plans. She uses her young body, strong, brown, voluptuous, like a weapon, like a grenade, to wreak her revenge because she thinks we don't love her enough, we can't. I won't be able to stop her. Even my mother's afraid. Afraid of Frankie's body, the raw, animal power of her daughter's want. Overwhelming. Devouring. So hungry, it excludes everything else.

~   ~   ~

In Vermont, my father fixes things. He drives new stakes for a fence, he takes the boiler apart in the basement and puts it back together, he mends the barn roof. Usually he's all right. When McKenna writes after Tet to say Saigon Duck disappeared, he starts sobbing. 'Someone made a good soup,' Ah Bing says. I slip the photograph he sent from Saigon into my top drawer, the photo of my father holding up Saigon Duck.

My mother says she always wanted to be married to a man who's handy about the house. But I can see she misses Hong Kong sometimes, the wet, the heat, the tangled green, the burst of red flowers in flame of the forest trees. She misses my father too, how he told war stories on the poop deck. How thin he was, wild, unruly, unpredictable, electric, like Frankie. She'll be happier when he's happy, when he starts taking photos again. We have our own war here: Martin Luther King gunned down, Robert Kennedy, sniper fire, burning, riots, federal troops, national guards, four students killed at Kent State. We watch television footage of Americans evacuated by helicopter from the roof of the Embassy in Saigon. Nixon visiting China.

My mother doesn't tell me what she thinks, what she misses. At the end of summer, she makes paper offerings, little painted jackets, school books, a bicycle for Ah Bing to burn. She constructs a tiny paper replica of our house, exact with its white clapboards, curtains in the windows, the front porch screened to keep out mosquitoes, the red barn with its mended roof, silhouettes of chickens, prettily painted, carefully cut out. She puts those in the fire too.

I float a water lily for Frankie on the pond so she can sail away on it like Kuan Yin to Hsiang-shan Monastery on the island of Putuo. She wears a blue dress. A silver chain around her waist. I float another one for the deaf boy and hope it reaches him halfway across the world. If I sit quietly enough, not moving, I may see a fish or turtle swim past in the murky water. A red-winged black bird will call from the rushes. A chipmunk might run across my foot.

I think about my father's question: 'If you are happy here, why wasn't Frankie?' I still can't find an answer.

forty-two

Before we leave Hong Kong, I go to the deaf boy's house.

'Fuck me. I want you to.' I say it quietly though I could scream. Fuck me the way Frankie was fucked. It's your fault too, I want to tell him. You should not have loved me. You should not have sought me out. I am invisible, white ghost, *gwaimui*, Viet Cong. I betrayed Frankie when I loved you. Because I loved you more.

The deaf boy takes me to his room with the rocks and shells and snakeskins and books. The room where we undress each other. A hot wind catches at the rattan shade, flapping it against the wall. Typhoon Kate, my namesake, is predicted to pass close enough to the colony tonight to bring gales and heavy rain, enough to fill Hong Kong's reservoirs.

Before he can touch me, I tell the deaf boy about the bomb at Lantau. We kneel on the bed, face to face.

'It's because of me,' I say. 'I killed a woman. I burned a boy. I dropped the lychees into an oilcan near the stall that exploded. I couldn't stop Frankie jumping off the boat.' I move my lips slowly to make sure he can see what I'm saying. He's the only person I've ever told. Then I reach out as if to touch the scars on the burned boy's face, the hard ridges of his skin. The deaf boy doesn't flinch. He doesn't look away. His face is smooth and wet. He cries for what happened to Frankie, what's happened to me. He doesn't want me to go.

Now I feel the whole length of the deaf boy's body, his skin soft, moist with sweat, the thin bones of his feet, the sharp points of his knees, the tautness of his chest. His body trembling. He desires me even if I am *gwaimui*, white ghost girl, a killer.

I loved you, Frankie. I lived you. Breathed your breath. Felt your leg thrown heavily over me in sleep. I followed your every scheme. Climbed jungles after you. I held my breath underwater for as long as I could. I carried a bomb for you. I listened to your lies and threats. Tried to clean up after you. I wanted to protect you, to keep you safe. I didn't know how. I was too little. I wasn't strong enough.

I press my eyes shut as the deaf boy pushes into me. I feel a sharp pain. In this darkness, my body thrusts up against the dead, shipwrecked bodies, floating planks. I am oily with spilled diesel, plastic bags catch on my feet. I cling to the deaf boy, clamber up him gasping for air. Cry out. It seems I don't want to drown, I don't want to be punished or killed after all, not the way Frankie was. I don't ever want to leave Hong Kong, this dark house, the room with shells and snakeskins. The hot, heavy rain pounding outside.

The deaf boy's body is beautiful. It's lean, thin, unformed, like mine. I'd like to tell him this, tell him I love him. That no one else will be able to give me the things I want.

I still haven't learned to say these things.

forty-three

Ah Bing feeds the stray cats. Dozens of them come every evening to the front steps of our new apartment. This is in Rome where we moved just as McKenna once suggested. She lays out saucers of the day's leftovers: pasta, mushrooms, rice, meat. They'll eat anything. She tends to them the way she tends the hungry ghosts. The cats are thin and scrawny. We call them by what is defective or missing: No Eye, Stub Tail, Bad Skin.

Ah Bing doesn't like Italy. She's only come to look after me. There are no other amahs, no Chinese supermarkets. She stocks up on ginger, dried oysters, black beans when we visit America. Or when she goes home to visit the temple at Mui Wo. She cooks me soup with ginger and lettuce. Her only friend is the Italian gardener. He doesn't understand a word she says but he listens, entranced by her operatic style, her repertoire.

~   ~   ~

As I grow older, the stories I tell myself narrow to one: it's the shadowy image of a Viet Cong, slipping back into the jungly, wet undergrowth at the back of a beach. Pushing palmy leaves aside, he pulls his loose black trousers up above the brackish water. I see where his skin is scarred, bitten. His gun's slung across his back. He's stuck leaves in his helmet. Leeches bleed his ankles.

Each time I follow, I go further back, wade through the murky tangle of mangrove swamp up into thick forest where vines choke oaks and chestnuts, wide palm leaves and sharp grasses grow out of rotted wood. The Viet Cong is always just ahead. Quiet. Barefoot.

One day, we emerge blinking among long straight rows of red trees cut into the forest, a rubber plantation. He moves fast now because it's dangerous here, exposed. It's like walking in an optical illusion because the way the trees grow you can see for miles ahead and behind but nothing at all to either side. A sniper could hide there, waiting. Still, I'm a good shot and I'm ready, alert. I'll be able to show him that.

Finally, the Viet Cong slows his pace. I stop to catch my breath. We've arrived in true highland jungle, where we can no longer see the sun, just the green iridescence of triple canopy, like being underwater. Here there is only the phosphorescence of rotting leaves to guide our way. The smell of hot tiger breath on my neck makes me shiver.

After all these years, this is all I want: a wooden stool, a bowl of rice, an army canteen, a secret comrade, the whooping cry of wild gibbons.

I would like to thank Les Plesko for his inspired and
happily irreverent editing; Felicity Rubinstein for believing
the book could be published; and all those at Atlantic Books.
I would also like to thank my parents for taking me to Hong Kong.

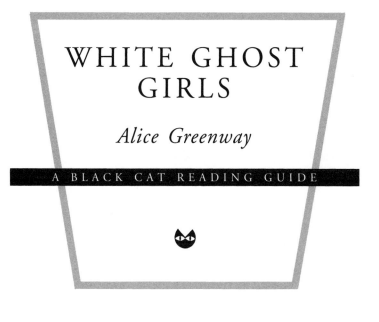

WHITE GHOST
GIRLS

Alice Greenway

ABOUT THIS GUIDE

We hope that these discussion questions
will enhance your reading group's exploration
of Alice Greenway's *White Ghost Girls*. They are
meant to stimulate discussion, offer new viewpoints,
and enrich your enjoyment of the book.

More reading group guides and additional information,
including summaries, author tours, and author sites,
for other fine Black Cat titles, may be found on
our Web site, www.groveatlantic.com.

WHITE GHOST GIRLS

Alice Greenway

A BLACK CAT READING GUIDE

QUESTIONS FOR DISCUSSION

1. In what ways does the narrator see herself and her sister as "castaways" (p. 2) and "Secret sisters. Shipwrecked sisters. Vietcong sisters" (p. 4)?

2. How are Kate and Frankie different, physically and temperamentally? How do these differences influence their relationships with their parents? "Frankie is faster, bigger, stronger. But she's also more needy. She needs my participation, my surrender in order to assert herself" (p. 5).

3. "Hong Kong would be safer than Saigon; an old-fashioned British enclave, he called it. That was before the trouble started this summer" (p. 12). What is ironic about their parents' efforts to keep the girls safe from the horrors of Vietnam? Why are Kate and Frankie obsessed with war games and following the events in Vietnam?

4. What is the picture of the war in Vietnam as it emerges in the book? What about America's role, and their father's?

5. How is Marianne, the mother, portrayed? Are there multiple facets in her daughters' perceptions of her? How does her art reflect her efforts to keep order and civility in her family's life? Churchgoing and tea parties? "I feel my mother wrap herself in it, the charm and comforts of the colonial era" (p. 29). What is her relationship with her husband? Does it change by the end of the book?

6. The father, too, is a complex person. Is he a good father? What are his strengths? His limitations, from Kate's point of view? Is Kate fair in her evaluations of him? Do you as a reader empathize with him as the book goes on? Explain his deep attraction to Vietnam. "It's hard for him to remember us sometimes. He loves Vietnam so much" (p. 49).

7. What is the role of Ah Bing? As amah is she an alternative mother figure for them? What kinds of worlds does she open? What are her memories of Mao and the Cultural Revolution? "Ah Bing knows we're no longer safe. From Mao. From dead bodies. From ourselves. We're changing too fast. We can't be trusted" (p. 18). How well does Ah Bing know the girls?

8. "The Chinese believe dragons lie curled asleep under these hills. . . . Then the great beasts must be appeased, offerings made, to avoid disease, bankruptcy or sudden, unexplained death" (p. 5). Death pervades the story from the beginning. Consider the shark threat in the harbor that turns out to be a body. "We're caught, rapt, unable to look away. It's as if we expect the body to roll over in the sea and speak, tell us her story" (p. 8). What is "the sudden change in everything" (p. 9) after they see the remains of the woman in the water? What are the deeper implications for their mother?

9. How does Ah Bing's temple on Lantau Island compare to the English church, St. John's? What does the whole temple world mean to Ah Bing? How is Kate particularly influenced by what she sees there? At one point she prays to the goddess of mercy: "Can you help me, Kuan Yin? Can you protect me from dead bodies floating up in the sea; from the Viet Cong hiding in the hills; from my body changing; from the lychees I carried, from Frankie?" (p. 133).

10. Describe the events on Lantau after Frankie induces Kate to run ahead of Ah Bing toward the temple. Kate says, "It's because I'm good at this. That's why they don't see me, run out and stop me. I've been in training. Hiding out. Playing Viet Cong with Frankie. . . . Camouflage, secrets, deceit, they're second nature. It's because I'm *gwaimui,* white ghost girl. I can make myself invisible, hide behind my white skin" (p. 62). How has the whole story so far been funneled into this one catastrophe? How is Kate's loyalty to Frankie instrumental in her actions?

11. The whole spirit world of Chinese traditions is a rich one. Can you recall specific details? Think of lighting joss sticks, fortune-telling, tending ancestor tablets so "they won't become hungry ghosts" (p. 69). Think of the mother carrying her baby in a special red scarf on her back . . . and the drugged moths considered to be spirits. Other examples?

12. Why does Kate have such trouble talking to someone about Lantau and the lychees? Even Frankie doesn't want to hear. "I think my mother doesn't want to know about me if I'm bad. It's why she doesn't look" (p. 74). How do the

lychees continue to define Kate for herself in the book? Who, finally, is the one person she is able to tell? And why?

13. As Kate tries to understand her family and her world, is she a reliable narrator? She tries to delve into her mother by looking at her paintings: "My mother's paintings are nostalgic, suggestive. They conjure a mythical past, an alternative present, one my father would be happy to indulge in if it wasn't for the war. A world she'd like us, her children, to believe in too" (p. 81). How is the idealized China related to the idealized old English colony? "Not this other China gone mad, slamming its doors to the West, cutting off pigtails, sending bodies downriver" (p. 81). Kate sees a further connection between Marianne's ethereal paintings and her mothering. What is it?

14. How does Kate roll Vietcong and Red Guard war games into her assessment of her own family dynamics? Give examples (see pp. 91–92).

15. One of the big differences between Kate and Frankie is their attitude toward sex. Discuss this difference. What are Ah Bing's ideas on the subject? Why is Frankie drawn to seek sexual thrills with someone like Humphries? Is it merely part of her reckless personality? Is some other need propelling her? How well does Kate understand her sister's behavior?

16. Since the father is a photographer, is it odd that there are almost no photographs of his daughters? Why not? What does one of the few photographs, taken by their mother, reveal about the two, dressed in cotton sashed dresses? "It's a testament to my mother's strength of will that she gets us

to church in this heat. The power of her sudden need to rein us in, dress us, render us up for God's inspection" (p. 20).

17. On his rare trips home the father's bedtime stories, as he lies on his back on the floor, are of Mao, Ho Chi Minh and General Giap, Genghis Khan and Marco Polo. Is this his effort to share his world of journalism? His trying to teach the girls to take their world seriously? What is the contrast with his Saigon Duck stories later in the book? "Saigon Duck's a magic duck, enchanted. A feathered Scheherazade spinning stories to postpone the day her head will be chopped off" (pp. 45–46). Does Kate inherit this gift for storytelling?

18. What does the deaf boy mean to Kate? He has a name, Fish Tze, but she always calls him "the deaf boy." Why, do you suppose? How does their relationship change in the book?

19. Is it the nature of a teenage girl to swing wildly as she judges her parents? "Maybe it's unfair the way I remember it. Maybe I'm too hard on my father. Maybe my memory exaggerates. Maybe he knew everything. He just couldn't help us. Like we couldn't help him. He hides in tunnels, behind his camera lenses, like I hide in the dark from Frankie, don't answer her questions, pretend to be asleep" (p. 99). Is it necessary on some level for children to protect parents to keep some coherence in their idea of family? To create a myth of safety?

20. Greenway creates menace from the beginning of the book. Midway, in a flash forward, we know some disaster is to befall Frankie. Is there a growing inevitability about Frankie's pell-mell behavior? Her mother says, "She's too wild, too unruly" (p. 105). Ah Bing, of course, agrees. "Why does she have to be

so demanding, so selfish, so present?" (p. 107). Could anyone have done anything different to protect Frankie?

21. How is the defection of the deaf boy's artist father a revelation to Kate? How does she draw an analogy with her own family? "I thought you had to take care of everyone. I didn't know you could choose" (p. 120). Is Kate's deduction on target?

22. How does Kate and Frankie's relationship change when their father is home? What is a defining moment when he tries to take Kate's picture? How is this event one more in a series of disillusionments in Kate's story? What are other times of loss of innocence for Kate? She started by saying this was to be Frankie's story. Is it? Is it rather both their stories? "I want to tell Frankie to stop. It's not worth impressing this boy. . . . You don't need George . . . or Humphries or Pym. Can't you see, we'll survive on our own? We've got the clothes under Ah Bing's bed. We've got our shacks of flotsam and jetsam. We're secret sisters. We don't need a father. We don't need to tell anyone anything. . . . I can't stop her from doing what she wants" (p. 139). Do you think Frankie feels as much a sister as Kate does?

23. How do you explain the last chapter, which stands as an epilogue written many years later? Is it Kate's epilogue only? "After all these years, this is all I want: a wooden stool, a bowl of rice, an army canteen, a secret comrade, the whooping cry of wild gibbons" (p. 168).

SUGGESTIONS FOR FURTHER READING:

The Whiteness of Bones by Susanna Moore; *Zennor in Darkness* by Helen Dunmore; *The Lover* and *The Sea Wall* by Marguerite Duras; *A High Wind in Jamaica* by Richard Hughes; *The Monkey King* by Timothy Mo; *The Language of Threads* and *Women of the Silk* by Gail Tsukiyama; *The Sea of Trees* by Yannick Murphy